BEWARE OF THE MOUSE

Leonard Wibberley

Beware Of The Mouse
Copyright © 1958 by Leonard Wibberley

New Paperback Edition Published by
The Estate of the Late Leonard Wibberley
leonardwibberleybooks@gmail.com

http://leonardwibberley.wix.com/author

Sign up for our monthly newsletter to receive columns written by Leonard Wibberley that were syndicated by newspapers nationally over his lifetime. You will also receive news of the upcoming releases of the ebook and paperback editions of his many novels.

http://bit.ly/LeonardNews

Cover Art Stock Photos by Dreamstime & Canstockphoto

New Edition Reprinting Proofread by Sharyn Essman

All rights reserved.
No part of this publication may be reproduced or transmitted in any form or by any means, electronic or mechanical, including photocopy, recording, or any information storage and retrieval system, without permission in writing from the publisher.

ISBN-13: 978-1518807763
ISBN-10: 1518807763

*Dedicated in knightly affection
by Sir Dermot of Ballycastle
to Sir Henry of Brentwood*

CHAPTER I

The year was 1450 and the day the twentieth of May; May the month of Mary, the Mother of God; the month of summer's promise; the month of the May dance and revels; the month when vineyards were painted with fresh green and hedgerows were bright with flowers; a month of laughter among people and of song among birds.

From the battlement of the donjon keep of his castle, whose walls rose eighty sheer feet from the courtyard below, Sir Roger Fenwick, third Duke of the Duchy, the principality and indeed the sovereign territory of Grand Fenwick, surveyed his lands. He could, from this eminence, see all of them, for the dukedom of Grand Fenwick, won by his grandfather, was but five miles long and three miles wide.

It was dominated by the castle on whose battlements Sir Roger now stood. The castle was perched on a mountaintop in the center of the dukedom and formed its hub. Around the outer walls of the castle were the houses and shops of the townspeople of Grand

Fenwick. These leaned against the walls of the castle for their support as their proprietors leaned upon Sir Roger for protection.

He was their liege lord. It was he who upheld their rights, he who stood between them and conquest by the French to the north and west and the wild lords of Switzerland to the east and south.

Sir Roger thought of these matters in the warm May sunshine and the thought pleased him. He was a man in his mid-forties, short, stout, red-haired as his father had been. He was strong of arm, deep-chested, deep-voiced and slow but determined in action. Every morning it was his habit to climb to the battlements of the donjon keep—five hundred and seventy-four steps of a circular staircase running up the walls of one of the towers—look about his little dukedom to see that all was well, and then return for a cup of wine to be followed by a ride around his estates.

On this particular morning in May, all seemed especially well. The vineyards, harshly pruned the winter before by his orders, gave every promise, in their profusion of leaves and tendrils, of an excellent harvest of black grapes from which was made the best wine in all Europe—the sparkling, straw-colored, invigorating wine known to all who loved their cup as Pinot Grand Fenwick.

In the eastern valleys were the grain fields, planted in the rich soil washed down the mountains of the Alps which ringed the Duchy. Here too the promise of harvest was good, while to the south, in the clear mountain air, Sir Roger could see herds of cattle and sheep grazing on the late spring grass, the sheep on the higher lands, the cattle in pastures rich with yellow buttercups. Away to the southwest was the Forest of Grand Fenwick, small but well cared for by the ducal foresters. From this forest came strong long-grained limbs of yew to supply longbows for the people of Grand Fenwick.

Every male from the age of eight to fifty was required to have a bow for the defense of the dukedom and required also to practice at the butts on Saturdays from prime to vespers.

The bowmen of Grand Fenwick were reckoned the best in Europe—the equal of those of England from whom they were descended. And since the longbow was without doubt the most effective weapon ever devised by man—capable in good hands of slaying an armored knight at three hundred paces—the safety of the dukedom of Grand Fenwick was in the opinion of the Duke assured.

It was twenty years since the French had made their last effort to annex the dukedom. They had come in three battles of a thousand knights to each battle, and charged, banners fluttering, dust flying, the ground thundering under their horses' hoofs, up the pass of Grand Fenwick. And three hundred of the bowmen of Grand Fenwick, arranged in harrow formation at the head of the pass, had loosed their arrows into them and stopped the first thousand French knights in mid-charge.

Then had come the second charge—a thousand knights again. And again they were stopped, again by the longbow. The charge of the third battle of the French had been a half-hearted thing. Sir Roger himself had brought down the French constable with an arrow through his breastplate, and seeing their leader fall, and viewing the havoc made of those who had charged before, the remainder of the

French fled.

The casualties were seven hundred and fifty of the French dead, and but ten of the men of Grand Fenwick. These ten had been killed by a few French knights who had somehow got in among the archers with mace and broadswords.

"Surely," said Sir Roger aloud, "the Lord has had us constantly in His care." He did not feel especially grateful for this, considering it to be the duty of the Lord to keep a special eye upon Grand Fenwick which was, after all, a settlement of Englishmen who had made for themselves a country in the northern European Alps and were thus surrounded by foreigners. Sir Roger viewed it as one of the functions of the Lord to preserve the English, particularly when beset by people who were non-English. Had anyone suggested that the Lord might have some regard for the French, Sir Roger would have put him down as a heretic and possibly a damned lute-playing Italian.

But on so pleasant a May morning, Sir Roger could not dwell long either on thoughts of theology or war. The land smiled around him. Cloud shadows floated over field and mountainside. From the booths and houses outside the castle walls came the sturdy noises of commerce and industry—the steady thump of the wheelwright working at his trade, the merry clanging of the blacksmith's hammers, the happy scrunching of the sawyer's tool as it sliced through a trunk of good oak, cutting out planks, and, from afar, the tinkling of cowbells as the herds munched contentedly in their pastures.

All was good and safe; strong and healthy. His world was exactly in balance. After fourteen hundred years of strife from the time of Christ, a perfect pattern for existence had emerged, in this blessed Duchy which he ruled. No man went hungry or unhoused or unclothed. No man went without his rights, scrupulously detailed under the feudal law. Skill at arms in the perfect weapon was matched by skill in agriculture and industry. No allies were needed by the Duchy either in war or peace, and God was undoubtedly in His Heaven and well pleased with matters in Grand Fenwick.

"By Saint George," said Sir Roger, "if others would but do what we have done here in Grand Fenwick, there would be paradise upon earth. Damn the French!"

He looked northward as he said this, to where the Pass of Pinot led into the French lands, and he saw in that moment a horse and rider approaching but so far distant that they appeared no bigger than a mouse.

Sir Roger studied the horseman carefully and then let out a roar. "Watch!" he bellowed. "Ho there! Watch captain! Blind your eyes! Don't you see that rider approaching?"

"'Yes, my lord," said the captain, hurrying toward him.

"Well then, who is he?"

"My lord," said the captain, "I have been watching him these five minutes. But the distance is too great and I cannot see what design he bears."

Sir Roger turned again to look at the horseman, who had just topped a rise on the gray stone road leading to the castle. The horseman, in full sunlight, was a little under a mile away now and it was possible to see that he was not armored, but carried a large bundle on the rump of his charger. Also he was unescorted and his horse was lame.

"A lone knight on a lame horse," said Sir Roger aloud. "And with his armor bundled behind him. He carries no lance and has no squire..."

"Possibly he is bewitched, Your Grace," said the captain of the watch and raised a pinkish, fleshy hand and crossed himself. *"In nomine Patri et filii..."*

"Bah," interrupted Sir Roger. "The English burned the last witch in Christendom with Joan of Arc, and properly too. That put an end to that kind of trickery at war. Wars are now decently fought on the basis of honest butchery, with prayers before and after battle of course. No more French tricks of appealing to magic and so on."

He looked again at the horseman, whom he knew must be coming to the castle. "I'll see this knight in the Red Hall when he comes," he said to the watch captain. "See that there is a loin of pork and bread for his trencher and a flagon of wine. Come! Send a man ahead of me! There are five hundred and seventy-four stairs to go down and I want all ready when I reach the Red Hall. Our knight will be with us, I judge, in twenty minutes."

Sir Roger looked once more at the strange knight and then left the battlements to go to the reception hall where he would receive his unexpected visitor. When he was out of sight of the captain of the guard, screened from all eyes on the spiral staircase, Sir Roger crossed himself. This was not because he believed in witches and enchantments but because he had become a little stout and could not see his feet in descending stairs. Any prudent man, in these circumstances, would summon the Lord to see that the Devil didn't trip him.

The Red Hall lay across a courtyard, under a portcullis, through an archway and down five more steps. It did not form a part of the donjon or main keep of the castle, where all retired in case of siege, but was in another building close to the armory, and adjacent to the main walls of the castle. It got its name because each of its glazed windows contained a diamond of red glass in the center, which, catching the setting sun, threw a red reflection on the reed-strewn floor to the delight of Sir Roger and his court. It was the custom to assemble there at vespers to see this pretty sight, to discuss the happenings of the day and to prepare for the huge dinner in the Great Hall which concluded the day's activities.

The Red Hall was tolerably well furnished. There were three backless chairs and, a special luxury, a large oak chair with a tall back to it. This, Sir Roger's chair, was placed with its back to the door and protected the Duke from drafts.

There were a number of niches cut in the walls, each with a stone bench upon which sacks of wool were placed for cushions. And on the inner wall, which had no windows, were four fine tapestries, depicting scenes from the chase. Altogether it was a hall of which many a king could be proud, and Sir Roger was but a duke, though owing allegiance to no man.

As he had half expected, Sir Roger found his daughter, the Lady Matilda, already in the Red Hall. She had put on a fur-trimmed robe of pale blue and wore over this a blouse of white Italian silk, tightly laced to show her small waist and her well-rounded bosom. Her hair was as pale as hay and she had piled it in a mass of curls on her head, all contained in a net of dark silk threads. With her was her constant companion, the Lady Janice of Mountjoy, a dark-haired, ivory-faced girl who had half the young bucks in Grand Fenwick scribbling odes to her. The other half, Sir Roger was fully aware, were scribbling odes to his daughter.

"Matilda," said Sir Roger, "I'm expecting a guest. I wish to see him alone."

"But Father," said Matilda, "I just want to see him for a minute. It's been eighteen months since a young knight called here and the last one was on a search for a nail from the True Cross and a terrible disappointment…"

"He was a divinity student at Oxford and out of his mind," said Sir Roger. "And I have reason to believe that this one is likely to be the same. The universities these days talk so much about God that you would think He was a member of the faculty. In my days at Oxford young men learned to drink wine, fight the townsfolk, use lance and broadsword, sing in chorus, recite a little Latin for culture, and…"

"…and distrust foreigners," his daughter finished for him. "I know. I also know that a university education these days is rotting the heart out of the youth of England, and that education should, in general, be restricted to priests who are protected from its evil influence by the daily recitation of Mass. But perhaps this young man has never been to Oxford. And, Sire, I am young...and a woman also."

Sir Roger grunted. Since she was five years of age and her mother had died, he had never won an argument with his daughter. He supposed she'd get married one of these days, and because the prospect troubled him deeply, he refused to contemplate it.

"All right," he said. "But you will leave after the introductions."

"If he is handsome may I sit next to him at dinner?" asked Matilda.

"No," said Sir Roger. "But if he is old and has lost a nose or an eye in a tournament, you may sit on his lap."

The door at the end of the Red Hall opened at that minute and the steward walked in and bowed first to the Lady Matilda and the Lady Janice and then to Sir Roger. "Sir Dermot, of Ballycastle, Your Grace," he said.

"Oh God!" said Sir Roger under his breath. "An Irisher." And then he called aloud, "Welcome to Grand Fenwick, Sir Dermot. Enter, I pray you. All here is for your pleasure," and he gave a sharp hard look at his daughter and walked, both hands outstretched, to greet the strange knight.

CHAPTER II

SIR DERMOT of Ballycastle was thin and long-nosed and slightly stooped and made no great impression as a heroic figure on the Lady Matilda, who had been brought up on the *Romance of the Rose* and other idylls. He had a long mouse-colored mustache, the ends of which projected like two tails of mongrel dogs, beyond the sides of his face. His hair was thin though Lady Matilda decided that this might be the result of much wearing of armor and so could be counted a point in his favor. But altogether she was disappointed in the appearance of the knight, and pouted to show it.

For his part, Sir Dermot, having grasped the two hands which Roger stretched out to him, looked at Matilda and her companion and his Irish heart rose.

"Begorra," he said, "I've been through Hell and arrived in Paradise, for 'tis two angels that stand before me. Such loveliness was never cast in human shape nor breathed human air since Eden's gates were closed to mankind."

Sir Roger gave a sharp perfunctory cough with the intention of jerking the Irishman out of Paradise and returning him firmly to the more substantial surroundings of the Red Hall of the castle of Grand Fenwick.

"My daughter, the Lady Matilda," he said, "and her companion, Janice of Mountjoy." The bow with which Sir Dermot acknowledged this introduction was graceful and deep and conveyed immediate adoration.

The Lady Matilda began hastily to revise her first impression of the knight and, flushing prettily, a talent with her which she could put to use at any moment, said, "You have ridden far no doubt, Sir Dermot, and are hungry. If you will be seated I will see that you are served immediately."

"Matilda," said Sir Roger, "it is without a doubt true that Sir Dermot has ridden far, and that being the case, he will not wish to be tired further by prattling women."

"Faith," said Sir Dermot, "nothing would please me more because for the past month I've heard nothing but the bickerings and grumblings of men at arms and knights and squires and bowmen and the screeching of tavern wenches fearful that they were to be overlooked in their beds…" He stopped and looked at Lady Matilda and said, "My apologies. I'd forgotten your presence."

"Being unaccustomed, no doubt, to the presence of angels," said Lady Matilda archly.

"Exactly the case," said Sir Dermot.

"Come," said Sir Roger, seizing the Irish knight by the arm, and taking him over to the table. "Be seated and eat your fill. And when you have eaten and drunk well, then you may, if you wish, talk. You are, I take it, from the wars, sir? How stands the English quarrel with the French? We get little news here, and most of it but tales to amuse the women and frighten children."

"The tale I have to tell," said Sir Dermot, "would frighten the women and the children and the men as well. For it is a tale of the opening of the gates of Hell and the destruction of all those who look beyond them. 'Tis a tale that but a hundred survive to relate, and the half of them no doubt clean out of their minds. 'Tis a tale to rock the world and shake the Pope himself upon his throne—a tale, in short, beyond all other stories of arms ever related in the history of the human race. I do not know that it is proper for the gentle ears of women-folk…"

"I will retire with my companion, if you so wish," said Lady Matilda. But the suggestion was in reality a plea to be allowed to remain.

"…I said nothing about the ears of angels," said Sir Dermot and Lady Matilda nodded her head gracefully, and settled back a little breathlessly in her chair.

"You begin well," said Sir Roger. "A cup more of wine and then let us have the full story, sparing no detail of any kind. Next to a hunt I love a good story of arms."

"That you shall have," said Sir Dermot, and drank so deeply of his wine that the rim of the cup pressed his mustaches back almost to his ears.

"You have heard, no doubt," he said, "of the renewal last year of the war between France and England brought about by the attack of the French upon the English territory of Normandy where the Duke of Somerset commanded."

"I had not," said Sir Roger. "What brought this breach of the truce?"

"The French have a queer idea that France belongs to them," said Sir Dermot, "and they maintain that the Lord divided France and England from each other by the sea with this in mind…"

"Damned impertinence," said Sir Roger. "The sea was put there to keep the French out of England, not the English out of France. But proceed."

"Be that as it may," continued the Irishman, "the French invaded Normandy and threw the Duke of Somerset back until he was last autumn besieged in the city of Caen and bawling for help like a lamb for its mother. He sent four messengers to London before he could get the ear of the young king and it was decided in council to send a small army over under the commands of Sir Matthew Gough and Sir Thomas Kyriel to relieve the Duke at Caen.

"I was meself in London at the time, seeking honorable employment, and hearing that there was to be an assault upon France, placed me services at the disposal of these two good knights."

"A commendable decision," said Sir Roger.

"'Twas better than singing ballads which I was doing before," said Sir Dermot with remarkable candor.

"We gathered at Southampton, ten caravels and three cogs, our banners, pennons, bannerets and bannerols streaming from masts and rigging, the Cross of St. George at the forepeak of all vessels, and the sides thereof made gay by the escutcheons of the four hundred knights who with myself had volunteered for this service.

"Our total force was of three thousand five hundred men of whom four hundred were knights as I have mentioned, five hundred squires, cupbearers and horse attendants, three hundred spearmen from Wales, and the remainder longbowmen from the southern counties of England."

"Ah", said Sir Roger. "Longbowmen. By St. Sebastian there is no greater weapon than the longbow and no better men than those who draw it! A cup to their memory," and he filled the Irishman's goblet and his own as well.

"To the longbowmen of England," he said.

"May they rest in peace," said the Irishman piously.

"No expedition ever left England greater blessed than ours though we were but of a small size," continued Sir Dermot. "And," he added, lowering his voice, "no expedition ever stood in greater need of blessing. The Bishop of Southampton himself said Mass upon a high altar on the dock, and we shouted our responses to him across the water so that land and sea were united in a circle of worship, and knight at arms knelt bareheaded beside common bowman in service to God.

"The wind set fair for France," Sir Dermot continued, "coming over the sweet English downs, and when we had stood from the shore I marked the little houses beyond Southampton and the sheep in the fields, the copses thickening with spring growth and the white gulls that followed us from shore, and thought that in all my born days I had never known a better one for battle. And so I composed, to while away the time, a lay or ballad of arms of but seventy verses of which the first is as follows:

> Gentle lies the land in the sunlight,
> Soft the hill shadow and valley bend,
> Bright the sun on the hilltops,
> Bright as shields of young warriors,
> Bright as the bones of the fallen;
> Bright as the soul that enters heaven...

"Did you say seventy verses?" asked Sir Roger.

"Yes," replied the Irishman. "They improve as I go along."

"Why then," said Sir Roger, "let us have them tonight at dinner when there will be a greater audience."

"Do you play the lute, Sir Dermot?" asked the Lady Matilda.

"As one in Heaven's choir," said the Irishman without a blush.

"We will have the lute tonight," said Sir Roger. "Let's get down to business. What about the battle?"

"The battle," said Sir Dermot soberly. He lifted his goblet and drained it and then, looking neither at Sir Roger nor Lady Matilda, nor the Lady Janice, but only into the bottom of the goblet as if all of human knowledge and all beyond human knowledge lay cradled in the bowl, said, "'Twas the last battle of the world, for it changed all things." He was silent in a deep moodiness for a full minute and the three others, so swift was the change in the Irish knight from exuberance to desolation, said not a word.

"The wind then was fair," said the Irishman, "and the sea as if enchanted. 'Twas as mild and smooth as a blue eye and over it we sailed like men journeying into a wonderment, and so made the French coast by evening. And still all around was calm and gentle as if all nature agreed with our venture—or waited the outcome.

"We camped on the shore that night and the following morning, all being still fair, set out for Caen which lies, as you may know, Sir Roger, not much beyond a league inland and up a small river whose name I disremember.

"Good Sir Thomas Kyriel had sent ahead of us a party of mounted bowmen and we were hardly well upon our way before these returned to say that a French army under the Constable Richemont and the Count of Clermont had interposed itself between us and Caen, at the hamlet of Formigny.

"All were much heartened by this news for we had not thought to have our sport so early of the French. The ground about favored battle, there being several orchards in full bloom in which our longbowmen might have cover while firing and, before these orchards, some newly sown fields in which the French cavalry might founder as is their custom."

"So it was at Crécy and Poitiers and Agincourt," said Sir Roger. "And so it was at the Pass of Pinot of which I will tell you later."

"I do not know, Sir Roger, whether you have much remarked upon the behavior and aspect of men before battle,'" continued Sir Dermot. "But I have made note of these matters myself and find them strange. For first among our bowmen there was some quarreling as to whether the men of Hampshire did not draw a stronger bow than those of Dorset and many came to fisticuffs on this point, while before us the French formed their lines, the Constable under the Lilies of France, and the Count under the standard of the Luces, and so in order of rank until they were stretched out in a line of half a mile, as bright as jewels, their armor glinting in the sunlight, their banners and surcoats brave splashes against the brown and green of the fields.

"And still our men of Hampshire and of Dorset swore and quarreled with each other and then, tiring of this, unwrapped their bowstrings from around their waists, bent their bowstaves and strung them, and then plucked them for test. The deep hum of this plucking reached over to the French and their lines were quiet, for I think fear was on them at the sound.

"Then these same bowmen dispersed themselves through the orchards, on the right and on the left, while we of the degree of knight were ordered to dismount and take the center of the battle afoot, for the way to kill a Frenchman is to kill first his horse, and this is best done with the sword beneath the belly armor.

"When all then was ready for battle, and the heralds had exchanged their courtesies, a deep quiet fell upon the field. A little wind had arisen from the direction of the French and this we took as a good sign, for it would give loft to our arrows and when they fell it would be steeply down between the armor joints and so do the greatest mischief.

"The French knights, then, mounted, were opposite us who were afoot. On their two wings were the rest of their battle, churls who dragged about what we took to be two faggots of wood and pointed them in our direction. These faggots were pointed at our longbowmen in the orchards on either flank, and we did not know what to make of them.

"We waited, then, for the French to advance until they had come within longbow range. But they made no stir toward us and the longbowmen jeered at them and cried to them to come on and be spitted or clear the field and let Englishmen pass unmolested on English soil.

"Then there came from the French lines a roll of drums and a high scream upon a hunting horn. And that scream, like the trumpet of the Angel of Doom, had hardly died away before there came from both sides of the French lines, where the faggots had been put, a great flash of fire, and a white cloud of smoke which was accompanied by a roar like thunder trapped between mountains. Then over our heads was a whining and a humming sound. Trees were snapped in two as if by magic. Men blossomed blood from chest and head and legs and there rolled to me feet the head of one of our bowmen, the eyes still bright with life."

Sir Roger crossed himself. "'Twas witches' work," he said, "they have found more of them."

"'Twas more than witches' work," said the Irishman. "'Twas Hell itself sent against us. For from these same faggots came another flash and another cloud of smoke and another roar. And then again the same humming and whining. And then again the branches of trees raining to the earth like nuts in an autumn wind, and men snapped clean in two, or their bowels ripped from them to wet the grass, or their bodies pulped to dog's food before me very eyes.

"And still the French had not advanced to within range of our longbows. They held these faggots of theirs, which they call cannon, a quarter of a mile away and slaughtered our bowmen as if they were babes in the time of Herod."

"And what then?" asked Sir Roger.

"What then?" cried Sir Dermot. "Why, the men of Hampshire called to those of Dorset to show *now* who could pull the longest bow, and bending their bowstaves in fury to the length of their arms and drawing the bowstring past the ear released a flight of arrows that sped like a flock of starlings out of the orchard. And this flight fell short of the French by two hundred paces.

"Then once more the French fired at our archers, and once more they were cut down and mangled as if a thousand devils were among them and tearing them to pieces.

"Then the longbowmen cried they would have no more of it, but since the French would not advance on them, they would advance on the French and pin them to the earth with their arrows.

"So they streamed from the orchard, and they were scarcely out of the protection of the trees, and had hardly fitted their arrows to bowstrings when the French cavalry charged with a great shout, their lances coming down one after the other like the sails of a windmill.

"We then, of the order of knight, went to the aid of our

bowmen who had but light bucklers and short swords for their weapons, their longbows being useless in the melee. The French came out of the sun in three lines of armor. The ground shook as they came and they rode our bowmen down, trampling them into the ground under the hoofs of their horses, or spitting them on their lances like plucked pigeons held over a fire for roasting. They used, besides the lance, the short mace and the broadsword, the spiked ball and chain and the war hammer.

"We knights, dismounted, fighting on plowed land which we would never have chosen, were flung back before this charge. And soon came from here and there the cries for succor: 'To Warwick…to Warwick,' and 'de la Pole,' 'de la Pole,' and all about cries and screams of men and horses and blood and earth flying thick as spume over the Kerry heads.

"I had meself, being landless, picked before battle a particular French cavalier whose coat was of three pickerels gules on a field azure, for I thought to make him me prisoner and through ransom repair me fortunes which were in the lowest ebb.

"Twice in the combat I was brought to me knees and saw the face of the Virgin smiling welcome at me. But I said to her, 'Mother, forgive me that I do not hasten to you, but you would not have me come without a penny in me pocket.' And so I was given strength to rise again and, pressing ever forward, got at last to this knight of the pickerels gules on a field azure and cracked him over the knee soundly to call his attention to the fact that I was in need of some of his money.

"He then, seeing me below his visor, bent forward to deal me a blow with his broadsword, but I was not of a mind to wait for it and so thumped his charger shrewdly behind the foreknee. You'll know something about horses?"

"Yes," said Sir Roger.

"You'll know then that the horse hasn't been foaled that can stand still after it is thumped behind the foreknee. So this French charger reared up and Sir Knight, off balance in preparing to separate me head from me life, was thrown back upon the ground, and me on top of him with an Italian dagger in me hand that I keep with me for just such occasions.

"'Do ye surrender?' I shouted at him, holding the point of the dagger through the bars of his visor.

"'What rank are ye?' he asks.

"'Why,' says I, 'I'm of the rank of Death and the Order of the Dagger and the degree of anger that goes with the two.'

"'I surrender,' says he, and so I helped him to his feet and off the field…"

"You deserted your comrades for a single hostage?" said Sir Roger indignantly.

"Me comrades," said the Irishman, "were all of them dead or fled by that time. When the two of us got up there was nothing around but dead and dying men and horses, and the squires were already going over the field looking for their masters and the heralds making a note of the nobility who had fallen.

"Of our bowmen perhaps twoscore escaped. Of the Welsh

twenty and of our knights less than twenty, I being among them."

"The rest were dead?" asked Sir Roger.

"Dead," said Sir Dermot, "and the greater part of them by far dead of the faggots or cannon that the French had used; dead as it were of standing before the gates of Hell which opened in front of them."

"The longbowmen were useless?" said Sir Roger incredulously.

"They served only as targets for the cannon of the French," replied Sir Dermot.

CHAPTER III

SIR ROGER FENWICK, when he had heard the tale of the Irish knight, withdrew to his own apartment. He excused himself somewhat abruptly, for he was not a man of much agility in manners. He said merely that he must think over what this terrible development meant.

"Faith," said Sir Dermot, "I don't blame ye. But I've already thought it over meself and decided upon what it means and what I shall do."

"And what decision did you reach?" asked Sir Roger.

"Would ye like to buy a good suit of armor?" asked Sir Dermot. "There's a hauberk of mail with only two holes from halberds and they in the back, an elegant helmet with barred visor, greaves and gauntlets, as well as a cuirass that has a dent in it but not in a mortal part..."

"Do you mean to tell me that you are going to resign the profession of arms?" demanded Sir Roger. He was conceiving a dislike for the Irishman, partly because he wrote poetry and also because he had brought bad news into the bargain.

"I am indeed," said Sir Dermot. "It has become too dangerous altogether. When a fellow a mile away can knock your head off without first inquiring your name, there's no sport left in it at all. I'm on me way to Italy to improve me lute playing and so set meself up in business as a courtier in a small way. I fancy I've the gift of the gab, as they say in the old country. Ye wouldn't be in need of me services, I suppose."

"I would not," said Sir Roger stiffly.

"And what about the suit of armor then?"

"I never buy armor from a knight," said Sir Roger. "I either take it from him in honorable combat or have my own armorer make me a suit."

"'Tis a strange world altogether," said Sir Dermot. "Ye'd think it dishonorable to buy me armor but honorable to kill me and take it off me corpse."

"I fancy that there are some differences between you and me," said Sir Roger coldly.

"There are indeed," said Sir Dermot, not the slightest perturbed, "and the main and principal one is that I was present at the Battle of Formigny and you were not."

With that the two knights parted, Sir Roger to go to his study and think matters over and Sir Dermot to take his pleasure being shown around the castle and then the dukedom by the Lady Matilda, who to quiet gossip, took Janice of Mountjoy with her.

She nonetheless contrived to become unhorsed in the Forest of Grand Fenwick, and Sir Dermot was granted the boon of massaging her ankle and speculating on whether what lay beyond the ankle was as desirable as that which he caressed in his hand.

When the Lady Matilda had thanked him prettily and assured him that he had a wonderful healing hand but there were no other parts in need of attention, the two went on their way, discovering Lady Janice of Mountjoy but a few yards farther on and looking for them apparently in the branches of a large beech tree.

Scarcely half an hour later, the forest undergrowth being thick, it was Janice who was thrown from her horse and once again, her ankle being hurt, Sir Dermot found the pretty thing in his hand, and indeed the afternoon went so splendidly that the Irishman decided a man was a fool who went to Italy to play upon the lute when there were instruments of far greater delight ready to be played upon in Grand Fenwick.

He resolved, therefore, on returning to the castle to be overcome by a sickness occasioned by the horrors he had seen and the hardships he had endured, and prided himself that with the aid of this sickness, and the ministrations of these two ladies (and such others as offered) he might extend his stay in Grand Fenwick to two months or more.

Sir Roger on the other hand spent an afternoon of the vilest sort. A world which but that morning had been perfectly in balance and perfectly defended—his precious and peaceful dukedom—was now but a rich prize waiting for the first French captain who marched up the Pass of Pinot with three or four of these monstrous cannon following him. Or so it seemed to him at the moment.

No longer could his archers defend the pass. They could be killed from beyond bowshot range. Then the French would come through in their hordes, over the pass and into the valleys, and he would be obliged to withstand a long and arduous siege in the castle of Grand Fenwick until the French army withdrew.

They would certainly withdraw, Sir Roger told himself, for fully provisioned, and with its own water supply, Fenwick Castle could withstand a siege of eighteen months. And Sir Roger knew that the Frenchman was not born who could wait eighteen months for anything—other than a woman. For such a prize, the patience of a Frenchman was a cause of wonder to the world.

"Bah," said Sir Roger, who had himself waited eighteen months for a boarhound, "the French are ruled by women." He felt momentarily relieved at having found something with which to denounce the French and elevate himself. But in a little while he was thinking once more of the cannon and the longbowmen, and wondering whether something had not previously been known of this weapon, or whether its advent was the foul fruit of witchcraft in which the whole of France was known to be steeped.

He struck savagely at a gong on a table before him and told the servingman who appeared from behind a tapestry which formed one end of Sir Roger's study to find Almin, abbot of the monastery of Grand Fenwick, and bid him attend on the Duke.

The Abbot Almin was a man of great learning. He could read

and write in Latin and Greek as well as in English and French. He was a cheerful Benedictine, fat and rosy-faced, yet of good stature, and had been, by his own admission, a great roisterer in his youth.

Despite his learning, he was no mere bookish cleric, but bent the longbow, took part in the chase, and was often seen with his gown tucked up in his belt of rope, fishing for trout in the mountain streams, and assailing Heaven with Aves and Pater Nosters whenever he had a good one hooked.

"Your Grace," said the Abbot on entering, "I hear we have company—an Irish knight. The haunch of venison, I fancy, might do for a prime dish at supper to be preceded by a score of excellent trout I took but this morning, using a paste of unleavened bread dyed with the juice of elderberries."

"Have you ever heard of cannons?" demanded Sir Roger, ignoring the proposed menu.

"The laws of Mother Church?" said the Abbot, closing his eyes and bowing his tonsured head as he pronounced the name. "Certainly I have heard of canons, but there are none, I assure Your Grace, prohibiting the serving of venison in the Month of Mary, though in those years when the glorious feast of the Resurrection—"

"I don't mean church laws," snapped Sir Roger. "I mean a damnable invention of the pestilential French which can destroy a longbowman at two thousand paces."

The Abbot looked blank. "I am not familiar with the weapon, Your Grace," he said. "But perhaps if I heard more of the story, I might recall something out of my reading."

Sir Roger then related the tale of the Battle of Formigny and how the English army had been slaughtered by faggots which the French called cannon and which had belched fire and smoke and death as if the gates of Hell had themselves been opened. He liked the phrase, borrowed from the Irish knight, and used it as his own.

"Ah," said Abbot Almin when he had done. "*Lucem video*. I see the light. Brother Bacon was right even in this."

"And who," demanded Sir Roger, "is Brother Bacon?"

"Was," corrected the Abbot. "*Requiescat in pace*. He is dead now a hundred and fifty years. But in his lifetime he was one of the great ornaments of the Franciscan brotherhood and was persecuted for thinking too much. It will not have escaped Your Grace's notice that no crime is more horrendous in the eyes of the ignorant than the pursuit of knowledge.

"Brother Bacon was one of those who sought knowledge, and in the course of his seeking, discovered a strange powder. It is composed part of charcoal, part of sulphur and part of salt of rock or saltpeter. These three, mixed in a certain proportion, and struck forceably with a hammer, one day blew Brother Bacon out of his cell—according to popular report though I am not convinced that this is true. It is known, however, that the mixture produced a great quantity of smoke and flame and released violence in the air as if a thousand gales had sprung up from nowhere.

"When Fra Bacon had recovered from the effects of this remarkable happenstance, he was called before his superiors and accused by them of entertaining the Devil to dinner in his cell, for it is known that Lucifer, when he appears and disappears, does so in a flash of flames accompanied by a thunderous roar and a great quantity of smoke and a violent wind. It was further remarked that the good friar's cell, immediately after the violent visitation, smelled so heavily of sulphur that it might have been mistaken for the awful entrance to that terrible bottomless pit in which the souls of the damned writhe and scream in their eternal agony.

"Brother Bacon, however, denied any visitation from Lucifer and explained exactly what he had been doing and offered to repeat the experiment for the benefit of his judges. These, however, refused the offer and released him on a promise that he would never again do what he had done.

"To this Brother Bacon made a curious reply. 'Your Reverences,' he said, 'that powder which I have stumbled upon, put to use in some weapon yet to be devised, will one day destroy the world in which we now live.'

"The powder, Your Grace, was from then on for many years called 'Devil's Powder,' and it was Your Grace's reference to the opening of the gates of Hell which put me on the track of the nature of this new weapon of the French.

"For many years the nature of 'Devil's Powder' and how it is to be made have been known among many orders of brothers and indeed by many men of letters. But the violence of the powder, once struck or placed in a container and set afire, has been such that for long no weapon could be devised in which it might be used.

"In short, this powder destroyed all around it, and was like a fearsome egg which, upon being laid, obliterated its own shell. Certainly the spirit of the powder may well be held to be devilish, for it is known that among devils the young spring from the parent a thousandfold, destroying. him but at the same time reproducing him so that he suffers in his progeny a thousand times the agonies suffered previously. Since this process has been going on since the fall of Lucifer there are now ten million devils—"

"Damn the devils," said Sir Roger. "Get back to the powder. This Bacon was an Englishman, wasn't he? Why didn't he turn his 'Devil's Powder' over to the English who would put it to use only in a proper way to maintain decency on earth and respect for your betters?"

The Abbot smiled. "I would remind Your Grace," he said, "that in those times there was no division of Christ's church into what are now called nations. All were the children of God and those now called French and those now called English lived as one family in the bosom of Mother Church.

"Therefore Brother Bacon could have had no thought of giving the secret of his 'Devil's Powder' to the English since at that time the English did not exist.

"However, there has been no great secret, as I say, about this powder. The parts of which it is made are known to many. Many have tried to put it to usages of war. I recall now that there are in the arms chest of the Tower of London two small weapons, called guns, which use this powder and which will throw a stone ball a quarter of a mile. However, I doubt there is a man in England now who knows how to work these guns which are, I would say, the same as these French cannon."

"Why were they not put to use against the French before?" demanded Sir Roger.

The Abbot shrugged. "Perhaps because it would have been thought un-English of the English to use them first," he said. "Or perhaps because they were new, for in England, as Your Grace knows, it is a mark of unholiness to try anything which is new. That is always left to others."

"The English will try it now," said Sir Roger.

"I doubt it," said Almin. "I think it is still too new. They will reflect that the longbow destroyed four French armies but the cannon destroyed only one English army and that a small one, containing three hundred Welshmen. Therefore, they will deduce that the longbow is still superior, and until four English armies have been destroyed, the cannon is not a weapon to be relied upon."

"Well, there's some sense in that," said Sir Roger. "One doesn't get anywhere by being panicked by every new-fangled idea that comes along. The longbow has been a good weapon—is a good weapon. I doubt these cannon will last. They're too new—too experimental. They're uncertain, you admit yourself. And then, now I come to think of it, Sir Dermot is an Irishman and the Irish are incapable of separating fact from fancy.

"If a small green caterpillar drops from a tree on the sleeve of an Irishman he will two days later assure you that he was attacked by a dragon of four heads, one blue, one red, one black and one invisible, that the dragon was a furlong in length and that he escaped from it only after a battle in which he was left with but a pint of blood in his veins."

"They are an engaging race, without a doubt," said Abbot Almin.

"Yes," said Sir Roger, "but as I say, they don't know the real from the fanciful. That is why it is so important for us to rule their country. You can't have a collection of poets, mystics and outright liars running an island next door to your own nation. Much too dangerous and disorderly."

The Abbot said nothing.

"I feel better now," said Sir Roger. "No doubt Sir Dermot let his fancy run away with him. Some foul trick of the French perhaps defeated Sir Thomas Kyriel at Formigny. But this business of the gates of Hell opening—I am persuaded that it's just a tale.

"Indeed, I begin to wonder whether Sir Dermot was present at the battle at all. If he was, I am sure he did not remain to the end."

Still the Abbot said nothing.

Sir Roger glared at him. "Well, Sir Abbot," he snarled, "have you no comment, or are you too busy with thoughts of fishing to give me your attention?"

Others might have quailed before the Duke's wrath but not the Abbot, who knew Sir Roger well. He knew the Duke's rooted opposition to any change; knew that he always sought to ridicule anything new, to explain it away and convince himself that it was not there. And he knew that it was useless when the Duke was in such a mood to interject any comment.

But now he judged the time to speak had come. "My lord," he said calmly, "you agree so perfectly with yourself, and advance such excellent arguments that there is no need for me to make a chorus supporting you."

"Well," snapped the Duke, "is not all I say true? Is it not true that if there were any worth in this arm England would herself have taken it up? And is it not also true that the Irish are notoriously an unreliable people, so that the molehill of one man's life is the mountain of an Irishman's?"

"Your Grace," said the Abbot, "it is one matter for a lone Irish knight to indulge in fancies, but it is another matter for you to do so. For upon you and your decisions rests the future of this dukedom and all the people in it. We have here a blessed spot in a torn world, Your Grace—a place of justice and of freedom and of independence, beloved alike by God and by man. Yet this dukedom might become as foul and stricken as any province of France, and its sturdy peasantry whining beggars followed down the roads of Europe by their starving whelps, if you deceive yourself in this matter of the cannon and the Battle of Formigny.

"Change does come, my lord, in the affairs of men, and only those survive who see and meet the change."

"You think then," said the Duke, "that there is some substance in the report of this Irishman of the slaughter of the bowmen by these cannon?"

"I think," said the Abbot, "that the part of wisdom is to hold an open mind on this report while looking into the matter ourselves. We should send to France, my lord, and see what reports there are abroad of this action and learn what we can of these cannon of the French."

Sir Roger hesitated. Every instinct in him, every fiber of his conservative character, demanded that he disbelieve the story of Sir Dermot, for it posed such a tremendous threat to the little world of his dukedom. But, as the protector and bulwark of his people, he realized uncomfortably he must go against his instincts and against his character and investigate thoroughly that which he wished so deeply to ignore.

"My lord Abbot," he said at length, "send two of your monks into France. As churchmen they may travel about without harm. Be sure you do not pick fools. Let them inquire about these cannon and this battle and come back with their report. And let them inquire also into the intentions of the French, for if they have some new weapon which they hold superior to our longbows, they will surely come against us again."

"The monks will leave this day, my lord," said the Abbot, smiling contentedly. He had played his cards correctly. He had encouraged Sir Roger to storm out his prejudices against innovation and now the true facts could be ascertained.

He made a note to be sure to have the monks travel through Lyons where the finest silk for a new trout cast could be obtained at a reasonable cost.

CHAPTER IV

THE significance of the Battle of Formigny, heralding the supremacy of gunpowder over all other arms and, as a result, a revolutionary change in governments and the organization of society, was lost for a considerable time in England in the politics of a court where a smile to the wrong person might cost a man his life and his castle.

Having fought the French for a hundred years, the English were just about to start fighting themselves for a further twenty. The Houses of Lancaster and York were preparing to assert on the battlefield their respective claims to the throne. France and French weapons were therefore forgotten for a while and when the English finally tried the new weapon, it was on Englishmen—which might be counted a point in their favor. Having discovered its worth, they tried it on the Irish, though a century later, and with effective results.

The English awakening, then, was slow. The French, in western Europe, were the pioneers, being first in the field with effective cannon and gunpowder. In the East, three years after Formigny,

Constantinople was besieged by massed artillery, one piece being of such huge size that a score of oxen were required to haul it into fighting position. The German principalities took up the new arm with interest. But in the year 1450, Grand Fenwick, like England, of which it was in effect an offshoot, found the greatest difficulty in facing up to the new facts of military life.

The reason lay not merely in the character of Sir Roger Fenwick III, the reigning Duke, but in the history of the country.

The country had been founded by his grandfather, Sir Roger the First, who had had the misfortune to be born the sixth son of an impecunious English knight. He had been sent to Oxford University at thirteen, but had been in danger of starving to death before he could construe sufficient Latin to earn his living as a clerk. From Oxford Sir Roger had taken away only two pieces of learning, acquired out of his own observations. The first was that while the pen might be mightier than the sword, the sword spoke louder, clearer and more effectively at any given moment and was likely to continue to do so. The second was that "Aye" might be turned into "Nay" and vice versa if a sufficient quantity of wordage was applied to the problem.

Sir Roger the First, seeking a livelihood, had enlisted in the army of Edward III in the middle section of the Hundred Years' War and risen rapidly from bowman to mounted bowman and then to esquire and knight at arms. Encouraged by this success, he had formed a free company of his own, selling his services to the highest bidder. It was while he was in the service of Charles the Wise of

France that he had come by his dukedom.

Charles had commissioned Sir Roger to take for him a certain castle and its surrounding lands, situated on the slopes of the Northern Alps, the lord of this castle having on several occasions sided with the king's enemies. Sir Roger gladly accepted the commission and chose for his army as big a collection of cutthroats, slitpurses, and hardy rascals as ever left an English shire for the coast of France. They all had one thing in common. They were expert bowmen and could split a willow wand, when sober, at four hundred paces. With these at his back, Sir Roger had readily taken the castle and then, instead of turning it over to his master, Charles the Wise, had proclaimed himself sovereign lord of land and castle under the title of Duke of Grand Fenwick.

None had cared to argue with him. For patent of nobility he produced broadsword and longbow and asked whether there was any patent superior to these.

"A Duke of Normandy became King of England with no better warrant," he cried, and so his claim was accepted by the farmers and small landowners of Grand Fenwick, as he called his dukedom. Three times the French had tried to recapture the castle and lands and they had three times been defeated by the longbow in the Pass of Pinot.

Since Grand Fenwick owed its origin and its continued existence to the power of the longbow, it was only natural that Sir Roger Fenwick's grandson, His Grace Roger III, Duke of Fenwick, should be unready to accept, especially from an Irish knight, a story that a weapon had been devised which outdated the longbow, and should demand more proof.

At dinner that night Sir Dermot was introduced to the nobility of Grand Fenwick, of whom there were two families—Simon, Count of Mountjoy, and his daughter Janice; and Egbert, Count of Azule, and his twin sons, Derek and William, both of the order of knight though untried in battle.

Sir Dermot marked these two men. They were built like horses, big-shouldered and thick-limbed, and towered above their sire. They had a surly look to them and never smiled at the Irishman but were at clumsy pains to pay what courtesies they might to the Lady Matilda and her companion, Janice of Mountjoy.

The Freemen of Grand Fenwick, also bidden to their lord's board, were presented to Sir Dermot. Of these there were a hundred, to which must be added their ladies, and they were seated at the board below the Great Salt Cellar to mark their rank as being common. A further and smaller salt cellar divided the freemen from the musicians, writers and other serfs. With these the Abbot Almin always elected to sit, as a sign, he said, that true riches and estate are not to be had upon earth but only in Heaven. Sir Roger had many times told him he thought this downright rude, but the Abbot would not be persuaded to sit above the salt.

"I must practice humility," he said, "for in truth, Your Grace, I am very proud. At times I am even proud of my humility."

"Well, damn it," said the Duke, "come sit with me."

"No," said the Abbot, "it is better to be proud of being humble than to be proud of being proud. People are not so put out by it.

Furthermore, among the musicians and the writers there are many worthy anecdotes told, though I often have to do penance later for listening to them."

When all the introductions had been effected, Sir Roger, as was his wont on such occasions, gave a spirited account of the establishment of the Duchy by his revered grandsire, said that he believed it to be the manifest will of God that there should always be a Grand Fenwick, and called upon all to ensure that practice with the longbow at the butts was carried out weekly as an essential duty of a loyal subject.

His address was received with applause from the nobility and freemen and even the writers, who were always polite.

Sir Roger then asked Sir Dermot whether he would care to tell the company of some of his adventure and Sir Dermot related once again the details of the terrible field of Formigny. His story lost nothing in being now twice told. Indeed, it seemed to Sir Roger that it improved and the company was held as in a spell while the Irishman spoke of the thunder of the French cannon and the orange and yellow flames which rolled from their mouths and the hum and whine of the gunshot into the English archers.

There was not a man present who could not visualize the scene, could not see the bowmen close-packed, pounded into bleeding meat, and see also the trees about stagger and fall as in a tempest and the earth flung upward in agony.

Not a hand, of all the hands on the table in the banquet room, stirred during the Irish knight's story, not a bench creaked and not a word of interruption was uttered. And when the Irishman had finished there was still silence, for what had been related was too appalling for immediate comment. It left the mind paralyzed, as men's minds are paralyzed when they have a vision of the end of their world and find themselves helpless to avert the fate.

Egbert, the Count of Azules and sire of the two enormous knights Sir William and Sir Derek, was the first to awake from the Irishman's spell. He was a big man and a gaunt one, old enough in fact to be grandsire to his own sons, for he had campaigned much in his youth and wed late in life. His hair was white and came to his shoulders. His eyebrows were likewise white and bushy and his mouth was pulled violently down at one corner from a sword slash received in a French ambush when the attack had been so fast he had had to fight unarmored.

"Sir Knight," he said, "I take it that you have been much about in the wars and so may answer my question with good judgment. Is it your opinion that Sir Thomas Kyriel handled his battle poorly on the field of Formigny?"

"No man could have handled it better," said Sir Dermot. "Not even Henry of Monmouth at Agincourt. All was done according to usage tried and proved—the bowmen in woods so they might not be ridden down by the French knights, ourselves dismounted to deal with the heavy French horse afoot, and a fine plowed field before us in which the French knights would be mired in their advance. No battle, Sir Knight, was better handled—or more completely lost."

"And the reason for the loss...?"

"'Tis as sure as death," said Sir Dermot, "we fought with weapons outdated, for we could not get within range with our longbows and were slaughtered without the fall of a single Frenchman to our arrows."

Again there was brooding silence about the banquet room. Sir Roger began to sense dimly that he had been wrong in inviting the Irish knight to relate the story of the field of Formigny, for what should have been kept private, at least for a while, had now been made public, and the men of Grand Fenwick, seated here at his board, were shaken, heavily shaken, and likely to lose faith in their honorable weapon, the longbow.

He looked at the Abbot at the other end of the hall but that worthy, of all present, was picking over the remnants of a pickled swan that lay upon his trencher and, satisfied that there were no gleanings upon his own platter, turned to that of Nicholas Breakspear, poet and chief scribe of the Duchy, who sat beside him. The Irishman was talking still, describing a breastplate of fine Italian steel he had found upon the field with a hole in it big enough, as Sir Dermot put it, to make a collar for an oak tree. Desperate to put an end to this kind of talk, Sir Roger arose, and bowing to his daughter, the Lady Matilda, announced firmly that she might be excused.

The interruption of the ladies' withdrawal, with Sir William and Sir Derek of Azule insisting upon escorting the Lady Matilda and the Lady Janice to the door, broke for a moment the gloom which had settled upon all in the banquet hall, except the Abbot. Sir Roger, determined to do what he could to repair the damage to morale of his subjects, said, when the ladies had withdrawn:

"Gentlemen, let us not be dismayed by this matter as if it were some thunderbolt dropped unexpectedly from a summer's sky to destroy us. Here is no new marvel which has been unfolded before us, but a matter known to learned men for the past hundred and twenty years or more. My lord Abbot is no stranger to this gunpowder or these guns, and can plainly tell you how this gunpowder came to be discovered and how it can be made."

All turned to the Abbot, who wiped his fingers upon a piece of bread, popped it into his mouth, washed the morsel down with a cup of wine and rose, strong, portly, substantial and unshaken. The Duke had never before felt so grateful for the mere physical presence of the Abbot.

"What His Grace says is true," said the Abbot, and related how gunpowder had been discovered by Friar Bacon well over a century previously and how the good friar had been blown out of his cell by his own discovery. He gave the composition of the gunpowder and those around the board started to cheer up, for the Abbot's Voice and attitude, his well-fed frame and his cheerful countenance inspired confidence.

When the Abbot had done, Nicholas Breakspear, the poet, asked leave to ask a question. There had been a good-natured feud between the Abbot and the poet for years. They liked to match wits with each other and play pranks on each other, and the Abbot had vowed on many occasions that he would not part from the world until he had saved the soul of the poet from the damnation into which it was assuredly headed.

"We know," said Breakspear, "of carbon, which is obtained by the heating of wood, and of sulphur of which quantities may be had from the volcanoes of Italy, and which is much used in time of plague to give the sufferers a foretaste of Hell. But what is the nature of this saltpeter?"

"Your Grace," said the Abbot, "I am asked what is the nature of this saltpeter or salt of rock which forms the greatest part of the mixture which constitutes the devil's powder or gunpowder. I will answer you straightly.

"Its nature, that is to say its essence, is found in the scrapings of stable walls."

Each now looked at his neighbor, uncertain how to receive this astonishing revelation—whether to believe it, or whether to laugh at it, or whether to remain silent.

"Sir Abbot," said the Duke, "I think you have drunk too well with your writers and musicians there."

"Your Grace," said the Abbot, "*in vino veritas*. However well I have drunk, I tell you the truth. Brother Bacon, the discoverer of gunpowder as it is now called, had many times experimented with carbon and sulphur in the hope of producing a spontaneous combustion but without success. His experiments occupied many months—nay indeed years, and he noticed that a certain incrustation was occurring at a spot on the stable wall near his cells which he had chosen for his convenience.

"He had, Your Grace, an inquiring mind, and so chipped off

some of this incrustation, distilled it in a retort and obtained from it a white salt. He mixed this white salt, which to hide its origin he called saltpeter or salt of rock, another name being niter, in with his carbon and sulphur. And it was that mixture which produced the explosion which blew him out of his cell."

Sir Roger was not yet sure whether the Abbot, who was of a roguish disposition, was serious. "My lord Abbot," he said sternly, "I charge you to answer me truly. Is what you say concerning this saltpeter true or are you jesting?"

"Your Grace," said the Abbot, "I have never spoken more truly in my life."

The Duke sat down heavily, his mind busy with some primitive arithmetic. There were in Grand Fenwick three thousand souls—in France, as close as he could estimate, at least ten millions. "We are lost," he said. "We will be engulfed by this abominable tide from France."

CHAPTER V

ON THE following morning Lady Matilda was early about, for she had not been able to sleep soundly. She had lain awake thinking of the strange, balding, big-mustached Irish knight who was so different from all the other knights with whom she had had any contact.

He mixed an engaging courtesy with a charming directness of manner and yet his speech had an extravagance that was almost poetic. He interested the Lady Matilda because he was patently no inexperienced youth who thought that a lady's heart was best won by breaking his own neck. Indeed, Sir Roger's daughter suspected that Sir Dermot, asked to risk his neck on her behalf, would point-blank refuse to do so. This was in marked contrast to the twin sons of the Count of Azule who were constantly vowing that nothing would make them happier than an opportunity to shed the last drop of their blood for the Lady Matilda or the Lady Janice. And she liked this contrast for she had never come across a knight with the mixture of charm and sophistication, roguery and naïveté that made up Sir

Dermot's character. When he spoke of war she heard the shrieking of the arrows, the clang of steel and the thunder of hoofs, and when he paid a compliment, he did it with a sincerity that made her feel that the world was void of women but for herself.

She dressed early in a houppelande of dark green velvet, trimmed with ermine and boldly patterned in a gold floral design. She did not bother to do anything with her long hair other than pass a comb through it and bind it with a ribbon. To have put on a call hennin or peaked hat with a veil, which would have been more proper, would have meant calling for her tirewoman, and the Lady Matilda did not wish anyone to know she was abroad so early. Hatless then, and unveiled, she went from the apartments she occupied to the gardens of the castle, where the first roses were now appearing, and where there was the sweet shy smell of morning violets, and the smooth grass was speckled prettily with apple blossoms.

She hoped that it was just possible that she might meet with Sir Dermot in the garden. Alternatively he might see her walking there, for the garden lay under the window of his apartment. But she did not know the Irishman and misjudged him in this. Nothing but a battle, and that within six feet of him, would persuade him to leave his bed before noon, and he snored away happily while her ladyship, growing increasingly vexed, pouted at the apple blossoms and the tight rosebuds, white and red, and wondered whether he was married. That he lay so long abed made her suspect that he was; for married men, she knew, took it as a right never to be abroad before their wives were up and dressed and the work of the household considerably advanced.

But though Lady Matilda did not meet Sir Dermot, she met the Abbot Almin, muttering his matins and holding a medium-sized earthenware jar before him.

"Good morning, Lord Abbot," said the Lady Matilda, a little put out by his appearance, and peeking to see what he had in the jar. But the Abbot had his hand over the neck, and she could see nothing.

"Good morning, my daughter," said the Abbot with a sigh. He was not altogether at his brightest in the mornings, and the interruption made him forget how many times he had already recited the Ave Maria and he'd have to start again. Sometimes he wondered during the course of his offices whether what he was doing represented religious exercises or exercises in mathematics.

"You are up early," said the Abbot, realizing this was the case.

"I could not sleep," said the Lady Matilda.

"Ah-ha!" said the Abbot, a shrewd man when it came to the Lady Matilda, whose upbringing had been largely entrusted to his care. "The Irishman. A witty dog, I'll warrant you. Just such a one as I was before I received God's call—though perhaps a trifle early.

"Stay away from that fellow," he warned. "He's Irish and a rogue, which is the same thing. Furthermore he's penniless and doesn't mind how he comes by his next groat so long as he comes by it."

"That's what I like about him," said the Lady Matilda. "He's a rogue and he doesn't care. Do you suppose he's married?"

"A score of times without a doubt," growled the Abbot.

"Do you suppose his wives—I mean his latest wife—is still living?"

"It's my view that he packed her off to a nunnery," said the Abbot. "We always get the rejects," he added sadly.

"I wouldn't like it if she were alive," said the Lady Matilda pensively.

"Tush, my child," said the Abbot. "Where does all this concern you? The fellow will be on his way by tomorrow morning. Sir Roger will see to that. He's an engaging rascal with a talent for telling a story. But we have no use for him around here."

"I want him to stay," said the Lady Matilda. The Abbot looked at her closely. He wanted to be harsh but he was incapable of being harsh with the Lady Matilda.

"Why?" he demanded in a voice which he hoped sounded severe.

"Because...because I think he needs someone to look after him," said the Lady Matilda in a rush.

The Abbot was taken completely by surprise. "Look after him?" he repeated. "That pot-walloper? That champion of the tavern brawl? That man whose smile would cut your purse and empty the pistoles out of it? That non-accepter of any challenge that hasn't a money prize to it? I know his sort, my dear. I know them well. He needs no looking after, though I tremble for the angel assigned by God to guard him. For that angel in the course of its duties must be taken into some of the direst perils and temptations ever placed in the path of a heavenly creature. What was that he said about the wenches of St. Germain? Oh, what a dog!"

"Nonetheless," said the Lady Matilda, blushing a little with vexation at the thought of the wenches of St. Germain, "I want him to stay."

"Well," said the Abbot, "Sir Roger will send him packing."

The Lady Matilda gave a little upward jerk of her head, an action which always signaled her defiance of her sire, and the Abbot sighed.

"Why is it," he asked, "that gentle knights, virtuous knights, those of saintly dispositions, all purity and prayer, never attract young ladies?"

"Because they aren't in the slightest bit dangerous," answered the Lady Matilda. "The kind of man I'm interested in is the one I lock my bedroom door against every night.

"Then why lock the bedroom door?" asked the Abbot, forgetting for a moment his position in the Church in favor of his curiosity as a man.

"I suppose because it would be too disappointing if I left it open and nothing happened. What are you carrying in that jar?"

"Nothing."

"You mean to tell me that you walk about in the morning carrying a jar with nothing in it?"

"Well," said the Abbot lamely, "I was hoping to pick up a worm or two while saying my offices in the garden. They are more plentiful in the morning."

"My lord Abbot," said the Lady Matilda, "do you think it proper to say prayers and peek about for worms at the same time? Do you think such conduct will gain you admission to Heaven?"

"I do," said the Abbot stoutly, "and that for the reason that he who keeps the gates, by popular account, is a fisherman. I have no doubt he had an eye out for a good fat worm even while in the presence of our Divine Master and Saviour. The Lord knows we are human and fishermen must have worms."

Her curiosity on this point satisfied, the Lady Matilda returned abruptly to the original tack.

"Promise me you will help me persuade His Grace my father to invite Sir Dermot to stay," she said.

"My dear child," said the Abbot, "you hardly realize the position you place me in, or you would never make such a request. As your father confessor, it is my duty to protect your shimmering soul and see that it goes unspotted (except for a minor blemish or two which is to be expected) to Almighty God. And then you ask me to help keep in our midst, in daily contact with you, a man whose very presence offers the direst hazards to your state of grace.

"My child, I cannot do such a thing. 'Lead us not into temptation…' It is the most poignant and trusting plea in the Pater Noster. No. It cannot be done. This is an evil roistering kind of fellow—though interesting. He must go."

"But," said the Lady Matilda, "is there no duty on the part of the true Christian to try to convert and lead to safety those who are going down the paths of damnation? Is Sir Dermot always to be condemned to the presence of the women of the tavern and the inn—the wenches of St. Germain? Does Mother Church forbid any other kind of women to associate with him? Is that Christianity? Are we to gain Heaven selfishly, ignoring the perils and struggles of others? Or are we to gain Heaven risking Hell—out of a Christian regard for the welfare of our fellows?"

"Lord, what a Pope was lost in you!" exclaimed the Abbot. "You could argue an Italian cardinal back to orthodoxy and the loving arms of Mother Church. Yet I am not persuaded that your interest is wholly spiritual and Christian. May I inquire how your ankle is this morning?"

"It is well. Why?"

"No trace of a sprain?"

"No," said the Lady Matilda, biting her lower lip and blushing.

"He has healing hands, this Sir Dermot," said the Abbot. "It chanced that I was fishing at the time you were receiving his treatment. Indeed, I had climbed a tree nearby, for in casting for a trout I caught my finest silken line in the branches of a wretched beech which I trust will be splintered by next winter's storms."

"You were spying," said the Lady Matilda hotly.

"Yes," said the Abbot. "I was. And it was prettily done on both your parts. But I know this approach from my own erring youth and you must understand what I mean when I warn you of the danger of this man."

"I understand only that however wicked you say he is (and I do not believe he is really wicked), I am a match for him."

"Ah, that is the refrain of the damned in Hell," said the Abbot, rolling his eyes to Heaven. "'I thought myself a match for evil.'"

"How do you know unless you have been there?" asked the Lady Matilda tartly. And then, suddenly, she was all repentant, coaxing child.

"Please Almin, dear Almin," she said. "Please say you will help to make Sir Dermot stay."

"He means so much to you?" asked the Abbot, suddenly quite grave.

"I don't know. I've got to find out. I'm all mixed up. But I don't want him to go. Not just yet. I'm afraid if he went I would lose him forever and I would regret his loss all my life."

The Abbot shook his head, not in reproof but in reminiscence.

"Even when you were a little girl," he said, "you were never contented with anything within easy reach; anything it was safe to get. You always wanted the nuts on the highest branches, the cherries on the slimmest twigs. Always the dangerous ones. Many a time I lifted you on my shoulders to get them. How long do you think old Almin will be around to see you do not fall when reaching for such prizes, little one?"

"Forever," said the Lady Matilda.

The Abbot sighed. "I promise nothing," he said. "But if any harm comes to you from this Irishman, I will destroy him and use pieces of his heart to bait my hooks with—may God forgive me."

This conversation had taken place underneath the Irish knight's window. He was awakened by the sound of the voices and clapped two pillows over his head so as to return to sleep. Then it struck him that the first of the voices had been a woman's, which was a matter of interest. And then he realized that this woman was discussing him. So he threw the two pillows aside, stepped out of bed and, a most unbecoming figure in his nightshirt, which had many patches, none of them expert, and his huge mustaches, tiptoed to the casement and listened unabashed to the remainder of the conversation.

When the Abbot and the Lady Matilda parted he stood stroking his lean chin and considering what he had overheard. He had on the previous day decided to feign illness so that he might have the Lady Matilda or Janice of Mountjoy, or with luck both of them, tending him. But here was a very different kind of stew, he told himself, and he had to admit that it made him nervous.

The Lady Matilda sounded suspiciously as if she were on the verge of falling in love with him. That was naturally flattering. But that was not the way he liked to play. Love led to matrimony. And matrimony led to an end to traveling about, taking your choice of the roads of the world, now feasting and now fasting, watching the clouds go over the tops of the hills and following them to see what it was the clouds saw.

It meant an end to tournaments entered for prize money and maybe a kiss or two, and an end to carousing in taverns. Indeed, from what he knew of the matter, matrimony meant an end to everything that was worth having and a beginning to many things a sensible man was a lot better without. Things like children. His friend

Sir Kevin of Rathgorm, who had been a pretty fellow with a broadsword or pot in his day, had seventeen of them, and what was worse, they were all girls.

Sir Dermot shuddered. To keep seventeen daughters virgins until married was beyond the power of any man. And it was well known that you couldn't marry off a daughter who wasn't a virgin.

"Of course," he said with his usual lack of modesty, "if I married the Lady Matilda I'd inherit a castle and a dukedom and that's not to be sneezed at."

He smiled for a moment at the prospect and then became grave, and there was a look on his face which was the first cousin to fear.

"Ah no!" he said. "I'm out of me mind. What would I be wanting with a dukedom that has the whole world to roam in, and never a tenant complaining about his leaking roof, or a farmer yelling because his neighbor's sheep got in among his new-sprouted oats?

"No, Dermot, me boy. There would be a terrible exchange indeed. Ye have the whole Christian world for your domain and maybe the Mohammedan world too if ye take a fancy to it."

The prospect of roaming the Mohammedan lands of which he had heard appealed immediately to him. "I wonder now if it's true that everyone of them heathens has fifty wives," he said, "and all of them walking around in thin baggy breeches ye can see through from half a mile away? A man ought not to go to his grave with a serious question like that unanswered. 'Twould worry his soul through all eternity.

"No, Dermot, me boy. No dukedom for you. Two birds in the bush were ever worth one in a cage though the clerkly sort would ever have it the other way around. I'll get dressed and pay me respects to the Duke and call for the Mare of Cashel—poor winded spavined beast—and I'll off to Italy and perfect me lute playing.

"And then maybe I'll go to the Mohammedan lands. 'Tis said the women have a soft spot for lute players."

So saying he started to dress, whistling cheerfully and wondering, since he was without a groat, whether he couldn't yet find someone in Grand Fenwick who would be glad of a suit of armor with a dent in it and a couple of holes and just a few pieces missing.

CHAPTER VI

THE news which Sir Dermot had brought about the new weapon that had demolished an English army had soon spread about the Duchy of Grand Fenwick. It was discussed in fields and in taverns, in smithies and saw pits; in tanneries and around the market stalls. It was the topic of the plowman and the shepherd, of the cowherd and the workers in the vineyards. It was a topic which everywhere spread dismay and awe, and although there were one or two who tried with a loud laugh or a cheery word to brush the matter aside, their efforts made them appear foolish in the eyes of their fellows.

This was an age when many wonders still were abroad in the world, and every wonder carried with it a heavy shadow of fear. It was an age when men could be burned alive for witchcraft (though no such thing had ever happened in Grand Fenwick) and when even animals might be sentenced to death because someone had reported that a particular dog or cow or horse was a familiar of witches. The minds of men were receptive to wonder and tales of witchcraft, and it was not long before the story was abroad in Grand Fenwick that at Formigny the French army had been commanded by a witch (some said Joan of Arc resurrected from the stake) who had been able to open the gates of Hell and out of them had erupted a blast of flame and brimstone which had destroyed the English, with the exception of Sir Dermot.

Some of those who listened to this story were inclined to speculate on why such an unprepossessing specimen as the Irishman of all the noble figures at Formigny should have been saved from these hellish fires. There were two theories—one that he was himself a familiar of witches and the Devil had spared his own; the other that Sir Dermot had visited the Holy Land and so stood in special Grace and the gates of Hell could not prevail against him. Before he had even arisen from his bed on the morning following the banquet, Sir Dermot then was a figure both of fear and reverence among the three thousand who made up the population of Grand Fenwick.

Sir Roger, like his daughter, had been up early that morning. He had climbed, as was his custom, to the top of the donjon keep to survey his lands and found the watch huddled behind the battlements, the soldiers talking glumly with each other. He hailed the captain of the watch, the same man with the curious pink and freckled hands who had first spotted Sir Dermot, and demanded to know what the men were discussing.

"Witches," said the watch captain.

"That's talk for children, not for soldiers," said Sir Roger. "I told you yesterday there were no witches left in the world."

"Why so I have told my men," said the captain, "but they speak of this battle and say that the whole of France is full of witchcraft. And it is known indeed that in the last hundred years not a single Frenchman has gained Paradise."

"And how is this known?" said Sir Roger.

"Why it is known," said the captain. "And that is all there is to it."

Sir Roger snorted, scolded the men of the watch by saying he would send their wives to guard the castle and they might stay at home and tend the spinning wheels and gossip like women, and then descended for a cup of wine and a breakfast of meat and bread. Then he mounted his horse and rode about his dukedom. But today there were few cheerful greetings from his subjects, whom he found in gloomy groups discussing the terrible compact between France and the powers of Hell, and many asked him about this compact and what might be done about it.

"Why," he told one group, "'tis no news that the French are in league with the Devil, but so long as we remain in league with God we have naught to fear." This did something to hearten this particular group, and Sir Roger repeated his happy summary of the situation to others and rode over to the butts to see who might be practicing with the longbow.

He found to his dismay but two men at practice where there were normally at least a dozen. They were Robin Goodspeed and Piers of the Glebe, and these two leaned on their unstrung bowstaves and confessed that they had hardly loosed an arrow all that morning.

"And why not?" asked Sir Roger, dismounting.

"Your Grace," said Robin, a tall, bronzed, curly-haired man in his forties, "you know that I come of Hampshire stock, my grandfather, who fought with yours, being from Winchester and as bold a man as ever killed a king's deer for his supper meat."

"I do," said Sir Roger.

"And you know that there are no better bowmen than those of Hampshire, for they have longer arms than the men of Dorset and other counties and this is common knowledge."

"So?" said Sir Roger.

"Well, I being of Hampshire stock and long in the arm and strong as well, have this morning tried my greatest range with my bow."

"And?" said the Duke.

"My shaft hit the butt at four hundred and thirty paces."

"A noble flight!" said the Duke.

"These cannon," said Roger gloomily. "I hear they throw their shot two thousand paces with ease."

The Duke frowned silently for a second. "You're afraid?" he demanded at length.

Robin spat deliberately on the daisy-speckled grass, wiped his mouth with the full length of his forearm and said, "I am Your Grace's liege man and would follow you into Hell. But I will tell you the truth on this matter and say yes, I am afraid."

"And you, Piers of the Glebe?"

Piers was a barrel-shaped man with the bowed shoulders and

somewhat bandy legs of a plowman, which was his calling.

"At the Pass of Pinot," he said, "when the French came a thousand strong all armored against us, I did not loose an arrow until I could see the rivets in their armor and smell the sweat of their horses."

"And now?" asked Sir Roger.

"Now?" said Piers. "Why now it seems that to loose an arrow is but to waste strength better saved for prayers."

"Do your fellows feel this way?" asked Sir Roger.

"I will not speak for them," said Robin, "except to say that they are men like us and have relied all their lives on the longbow and now do not know where to turn. Those I have talked with are of the opinion that we can expect the French—and soon. And they will come against us with these cannon and that will be the end."

"And yet," said Sir Roger, "it may be that all this talk of the French cannon is but a tale of this Irish knight and that in fact these cannon are more dangerous to those who use them than to those they are used against. My lord Abbot, who is as learned a man as you will find between here and London, holds this view himself."

"Ah," said Robin, "and what other view could he rightly hold, Your Grace? 'Tis certain he could not say that the French now overmatch us and our time in Grand Fenwick is ended, and we may no longer stand against the French king."

Piers of the Glebe bobbed his round head in agreement. "I fear for my children," he said. "'Tis a good life I've had here, Your Grace, and a pleasant land. But my children will not taste it as vassals of the

French king. Five acres of my own land I've plowed every winter, and every summer these five acres have given me my bread and wine, and a side of bacon on Sundays. But my children will not know this content, for it is certain the French will take their land and make them serfs."

"Before God," said Sir Roger, "they must first kill me."

"Ah," said Piers, "and me likewise. But kill us they will and likely our families unless we find some way to treat with them."

"I will not treat with them," said Sir Roger. "These are my lands and I will hold them while there is breath in me—against Hell itself."

When he got back to the castle it was noon and he had found that in the face of the new weapon a spirit of defeat was common in Grand Fenwick. All were in awe of the cannon against which they felt there was no protection, and Sir Roger called the Abbot to the Red Hall to consult with him.

"My lord Abbot," he said, "it seems that this French weapon has already half destroyed our people, for they are convinced that they cannot stand against it; and that being the case, I do not know how my army will behave when the French come up the Pass of Pinot with half a dozen of these cannon, as they will without a doubt. Some might stand firm and make trial of the matter. But the half at least will, I fear, flee into Switzerland and over the mountain passes into Italy, and fear itself will lose us this dukedom."

The Abbot sighed. "I was fearful of such an effect when I heard the Irishman talk at the banquet last night," he said.

"Damn the Irish knight," snorted Sir Roger vehemently. "It

was the Devil sent him here. But yesterday morning, before he came, this was an Eden on earth. Now the place is full of fear and men count the days of happiness left to them."

"Your Grace," said the Abbot, "I would differ with you. 'Twas the Lord directed him our way, for he has given us timely warning of this armament of the French. Better to know of it in advance than to have the first news by their opening fire upon our archers as they did at Formigny. What we need now is a diversion to take people's minds off the matter and time in which to consider our plans."

Sir Roger got up abruptly.

"What we need now," he said, "is a cannon. We need a cannon so that we may tell our people we have the same weapon as the French. One cannon here in Grand Fenwick would give them back their heart, and without heart all is lost. The French, as I said, have already half defeated us without striking a blow."

"Your Grace," said the Abbot, "I would suggest that you call a meeting of the Council of Freemen at which to freely discuss this crisis in our affairs. Let the meeting be summoned for three weeks hence, by which time the two friars I have sent into France will have reported on the truth of this Battle of Formigny. And in the meantime let us arrange some diversion for the people which will take their minds off this subject which grows the more fearful the more it is thought upon."

"What kind of a diversion?" asked the Duke.

"I have in mind a tournament, Your Grace," said the Abbot. "Mother Church does not frown upon tournaments, holding that they provide a method of releasing warlike spirits which might otherwise work to evil ends."

"What kind of a tournament could we hold in Grand Fenwick with but two knights, the twin sons of the Count of Azule, to grace the list?"

"Your Grace forgets that we have a third knight in Grand Fenwick now," said the Abbot.

"You mean Sir Dermot?" asked the Duke.

"The same," replied the Abbot smoothly. "On my way here I said a word or two in the right place and believe that he must either fight or flee. If he fights he will be killed and if he flees we are rid of him, and so no harm will come to the Lady Matilda whose sweet soul I have taken in my special charge."

"Bah," said Sir Roger. "Unless I greatly misjudge him that Irishman will flee. His courage is all in his tongue. A knight who seeks to sell his armor is a disgrace to chivalry."

"Whatever the outcome," said the Abbot, "we will profit from it. And as to other encounters at our tournament, I would propose that we proclaim a Truce of God for this event. Such a truce, as Your Grace knows, is binding upon all Christendom and no war nor plans of war may be made against us while it lasts. This would give us time to hear from our friars and consider our position in view of the French threat. And under the truce we could invite French and Italian and Swiss knights to grace our tourney, so we would not lack for contestants in the field."

Sir Roger began to warm to the idea. There was a distinct

advantage to Grand Fenwick in proclaiming a Truce of God for a month for the tournament. He would make one of the events of the tournament a longbow contest and would give as a prize a purse of crowns. That would stimulate interest again in practice, and in any case he loved a tournament. Mental effort of any kind made Sir Roger sad, for he believed himself so constituted that, called upon to use his mind, evil humors collected in his liver. On the other hand, physical exercise cleared his liver but prevented anything from settling in his mind to its detriment. It would put him in the best of health then to enter the lists himself.

"Good my lord Abbot," he said, rubbing his hands together with zest. "Have Christ's Cross erected at our frontiers so that all may know that a Truce of God is now proclaimed in Grand Fenwick. Send heralds to France and Switzerland and Italy to proclaim our tournament and invite the chivalry of these countries to contest in our lists. And I will myself enter the lists against the noblest Frenchman who attends. The exercise will benefit my liver and the challenge will benefit my subjects. See that the Count of Chaux de Fonds gets express invitation to attend. I owe him a blow on the casque for hanging one of my foresters who strayed into his lands in legitimate pursuit of a deer."

The Abbot smiled to see his lord put in such good humor at the prospect of a tournament.

"All will be done as you wish, Your Grace," he said. "But touching the matter of the Count of Chaux de Fonds, let it be borne in mind that the blows given in a tournament should be delivered with Christian charity and a desire to serve God."

"Whoever puts a dent in a Frenchman's skull serves God most handsomely," said the Duke.

Sir Dermot, in the meantime, having dressed and had a leisurely breakfast, and then spent some hours trying to sell his armor that he might have some money for his journey to Florence, went at last to the stables to set out upon his way. He had sought to take leave of Sir Roger but learned that he was in conference with the Abbot, and not wishing to spend another day in the Duchy or to set out with night approaching, decided to forgo his adieus.

The vision of the trap of matrimony which he saw plainly before him, threatening to put an end to his roving, had not faded and he was anxious to get out of the Duchy though concerned at being without a farthing in his purse. At the stables he called the groom, a lad of sixteen, and bade him saddle his horse, the Mare of Cashel. But the groom said the horse was still lame in the foreleg and could not travel that day.

"Well then," said the knight, "saddle me another. I will leave the Mare of Cashel here in exchange, for I must be out of the Duchy within an hour."

"Aha," said the groom, "you have met with Sir Derek of Azule?"

"I met him at dinner last night," said Sir Dermot. "What has that got to do with it?"

"You have not met him this day?"

"No."

"Well," said the groom, "I'll saddle you a horse and if you go out the back way maybe you can avoid him."

"And why the devil should I avoid him?" asked Sir Dermot.

"Why," said the groom, "he was here but half an hour since to look over his charger, and swearing that it must be fed nothing but oats and oil cake and put in the wildest and finest condition, for he is determined to challenge you to a fight to the death."

"What for—in the name of all that is holy?" demanded the Irishman.

"For making too free with the Lady Matilda whom he has vowed to protect."

"Lord," said the Irishman, "will the day never come that I may touch a woman on the ankle without having to fight half the knights in Christendom? Tell me, have you never touched a wench on the ankle?"

"Yes," said the young groom grinning.

"And did you ever have to fight about it?"

"Never," said the groom.

"By St. Patrick," said Sir Dermot, "what a fool I was to accept the degree of knight, for it has cut me off from all the natural pleasures of the world. And where is Sir Derek at this moment?"

"He'll be in the armory no doubt, practicing with the broadsword."

"Ah well," said Sir Dermot, "I'm a peaceable body. Saddle me a horse and I'll leave him to his practice."

"You say well," said the groom, "for there is no better man with the broadsword, mace, war hammer or spear than Sir Derek. Unless it is his brother, Sir William."

At that moment Sir William came into the stables, caught sight of Sir Dermot, let out a bellow of anger, ran to him and struck him over the face with his glove.

"I give you challenge, false knight," he said.

"You're late," said Sir Dermot. "Your brother has first call."

"I do not refer to the Lady Matilda," said Sir William, "but to that spotless dove of the mountains, the Lady Janice of Mountjoy whose honor you have offended by laying your hand I blush to say where."

"You blush prettily readily for a man of your age," said Sir Dermot. "But what is the Lady Janice of Mountjoy to you?"

"I am her champion," said Sir William, "and have sworn to have the life of any who offend her. Do you pick up my gage?"

"Tell me," said Sir Dermot, "you are the champion of the Lady Janice and your brother is the champion, it seems, of the Lady Matilda. Are there any ladies under thirty in the dukedom who are without their champions?"

"No," said Sir William. "These are the only two ladies in the dukedom."

"That being the case," said the Irishman, picking up the knight's glove and tucking it in his belt, "I suppose it was inevitable."

When Sir William had gone the groom turned to Sir Dermot.

"Shall I saddle your horse?" he asked. "You may still leave and none will know of it outside the Duchy which is a small place."

"No," said Sir Dermot. "I came here in peace and find meself twice challenged, and I've a mind to stay despite the hazard."

"There's hazard aplenty in a challenge from Sir William and Sir Derek," said the groom.

"I was thinking," said Sir Dermot, "of the Lady Matilda, may the saints preserve me."

CHAPTER VII

"YOU ask my advice," said Nicholas Breakspear. "I give it to you in one word. Flee. Turn varlet and quit Grand Fenwick. Those two oxen, Sir Derek and Sir William, will not leave enough of you to warrant burial.

"Be quit then of Grand Fenwick. But take me with you—as squire perhaps, or troubadour, or page or what you will. I sicken of this place. There is not a nimble wit apart from the Abbot in the whole duchy; and the Abbot and I are the only two (with the exception of a few of the monks) who can read within its narrow boundaries.

"I long for Florence. Ah, that sunlight; the flowers, the wine, the laughter. And the women. Flee then, and I will go with you."

"If you are so heartsick for Florence," said Sir Dermot suspiciously, "why have you not gone there by yourself long since?"

"Why?" cried Breakspear. "For a very simple reason. I am a craven. A coward. A cheese mite when it comes to fighting. Such men as I are needed in the world, Sir Knight. Do not doubt it for a moment. There must be cowards, for if all were brave, then bravery would be a commonplace and draw no praise. We cowards are necessary to heroes—the pedestals upon which the heroes stand. And I am indeed a coward. It has saved my neck many a time, and a man must save his neck as best he can.

"A coward like myself, then, could not brave the road to Florence alone. I need a hero to ride beside me, and when we are beset, as we will be without a doubt, I will add to your triumphs by fleeing on the moment.

"After the combat, I will write a poem celebrating the courage of the victor, which will without a doubt be yourself, and saying how you were left alone to face insurmountable odds.

"You see, Sir Knight, I can be of great service to you on the road to Florence. And when we are arrived there, the account I will give of your deeds will bring you to the notice of the greatest princes of the country, and win you high place in their courts."

"Well," said Sir Dermot, "'tis a pretty thought. And it may be that some day we will put this plan to use. But this is not the advice I came seeking, for I am a prudent man meself, and was all ready yesterday afternoon to slip out when in came Sir William, wild as the Brown Bull of Ulster, and threw down his gauntlet. And but a moment later—or leastways within the hour—he was followed by his brother, Sir Derek, who paid me the same compliment. And so I must stay and fight them."

"If I were you, I would still flee," said Breakspear.

"If you were me, you would not have been found out in this little affair of the ankles," said Sir Dermot. "And now that I come to think of it, I do not know how I was found out meself. Unless the ladies happened to mention it."

"It was the Abbot," said Breakspear.

"The Abbot?" echoed the Irishman.

"No greater rogue ever wore penitent's cloth," said the poet. "He has without a doubt some reason for mentioning the affair of the ankles to Sir Derek and Sir William. It is my belief that he wishes you dead and therefore you should flee. This Abbot of ours was trained in his youth by Lucifer, which makes him the more dangerous as a pillar of the church. For he has the cunning of the Devil welded to the purposes of the Archangel Michael. He would have you dead—no doubt to protect the Lady Matilda—and so arranges your death in this tournament with Sir William or Sir Derek—for whichever you first meet will certainly kill you—and he consoles his principles by maintaining that since God protects the right, you could not be killed in the tournament unless you were wrong. Take my advice and flee to Florence, and I will accompany you."

"And why are you so anxious for Florence—is it only the women and the flowers and the sunshine, or is there some other reason?"

"Sir Knight," said Breakspear, "I have heard that you can write?"

"I can," said the Irishman.

"And I have heard also that you can contrive a verse or two of some worth?"

"That is so."

"Also that you play upon the lute?"

"Agreed."

"Sir Knight, all these things I do myself, and with some degree of skill. Does not this then make us peers one of the other?"

"It does," said Sir Dermot.

To his astonishment he saw that Breakspear's face had gone an ashen gray and the poet was trembling as if with fear.

"Then, Sir Dermot, putting aside your degree of knight and looking only to your accomplishments as a poet and writer and lutanist, I am within my rights to challenge you, am I not? For poets may have their rights as well as knights. Is this not so?"

"Challenge me?" said Sir Dermot. "In God's name why?"

"Ah, gentle knight," said the poet, "you wronged me when you laid your hand upon the Lady Janice for I do love her more than ever man loved maid."

"I did not know this," said Sir Dermot. "Have you spoken to her of your love?"

"I?" cried the trembling Breakspear. "I? I who shiver here before you because I must strike you for love of my lady? I who am all love and all coward, a heart without strength, a voice without manhood? No. I could never tell her that I love her. Did she but move one eyelid in scorn, did she but smile slightly at me in pity, I would be destroyed in that moment. I love and I fear and these two tear at me like tigers over meat. And so must I go to Florence and seek there to forget that I love her and to forget that I am not a man, and being no man, am unworthy even to speak her name."

"And yet," said Sir Dermot softly, "you spoke of striking me for your lady's honor."

"I did," said Breakspear, his face ashen again. "Forgive me. But I did."

"Then strike, man," said the Irishman.

"I cannot, I am afraid."

"If you love your lady, strike."

The poet closed his eyes, stiffened himself and slapped the Irishman across the face with the back of his hand. Then he remained, still tense with his eyes closed, standing before Sir Dermot.

"Be done with me, Sir Knight," he said at length. "Strike back and lay my length upon the floor."

"Never," said the Irishman. "That was as brave and as honorable a blow as was ever offered me and I would not disgrace meself by returning it. Pluck up your heart, poet. The world is not full of bullies like the twin knights of Azule. We will not go to Florence, either of us. There are matters to detain us here.

"And now," he continued, "since you have no advice to offer me on whether to accept first the challenge of Sir Derek or Sir William—in short, which would be the easier to dispatch and so intimidate the other—I will be on my way."

"Where?" asked Breakspear.

"To the Abbot," replied the Irishman.

"I will go with you," said the poet with sudden resolution, "for if you will not flee but rather will stay and fight, this will be the greatest affair at arms that has stirred Grand Fenwick in many years, and I must know all the details. After you are killed, I will write an elegant and graceful chronicle of it, or perhaps a poem in epic form, and you will be more famous stinking in your grave than you ever were, fresh meat upon your horse.

"The Abbot will be fishing in the Lady Deep," continued the poet. "I will bring some bread and cheese and a little wine."

The poet had his quarters in the wall of the castle, and it was there that this conference had taken place. Their way now led them past the armory, from which there came the most prodigious thumping and thwacking and clanging of steel.

Sir Dermot peeped through the door and saw Sir Derek and Sir William, both padded to the size of giants, though in truth they were giants unpadded, thwacking away at each other with broadswords. Sir Dermot shuddered and the poet saw him.

"I know the road to Florence well," he whispered. "I have traveled it, though always in company, three times."

"The devil take the road to Florence," said Sir Dermot. "I shivered at the thought of that much exercise before noon."

They found the Abbot, his gown tucked into his belt, standing knee-deep in the waters of the Lady Deep, a small lake in the Forest of Grand Fenwick, and fishing for trout among the lily pads.

"Ho there," roared Sir Dermot when he caught sight of him. "If it were not for your cloth I would upend you in the lake and your bright nose would attract more fish than your red bait."

The Abbot crossed himself, cast his eyes up to Heaven and said, "Lord, be my witness. That was the third nibble I had this day and each one frightened off by a roaring fool." He turned around to face the knight and said, "What is it you want?"

"I want to know," said Sir Dermot, "why it is that you have set those two oafs of Azule upon me, that never missed a Mass in all me days."

"I had good and sufficient reasons," replied the Abbot.

"You do not deny it, then?"

"Deny it?" said the Abbot. "No. I do not deny it at all. But why are you not hastening down the road to Florence like a sensible man? We have little burying ground left in Grand Fenwick, and none for strangers."

"By the Seven Wounds of the Crucified Christ," said Sir Dermot, "everybody seems remarkably anxious to be rid of me this morning. Here are you inquiring why I am not for Florence and the poet was so anxious to set me upon the road he offered to accompany me, and I recall the groom was likewise persuasive."

"It is only that we wish you well," said Breakspear. "And what the Abbot says is true. We have little burying ground for the nobility in Grand Fenwick. And, sir, with your large mustaches, I do not think you would make a noble corpse."

"You are mightily confident that I would be killed," the Irishman said.

"Do you doubt that the sun will rise tomorrow?" asked the Abbot. "Let me inform you of something of the prowess of these two knights of Azule. Sir William, when angered, has been known to bend the breastplate of a suit of good German armor with his clenched fist. And the spear which Sir Derek, his brother, uses in a tournament is twenty feet long and weighs sixty pounds. Yet he couches it as if it were a feather. No two such men have ever entered the lists before in all the history of jousting."

"It should be a notable joust then," said Sir Dermot.

The Abbot snorted. "If an elephant kills an ant, the word for the deed is not notable," he said. "Insignificant would serve."

"Ah," said Sir Dermot. "But if the elephant kills an elephant—what then is the word?"

"You think yourself an elephant?" sneered the Abbot. "Why, you are the figure of a knight who fills his armor so ill that when he is clad in his battle steel he is two feet taller than before he put it on. I believe you sight through a hole in the breastplate, and your helmet is as empty as your head appears to be."

"You take me wrongly," said Sir Dermot. "I am no elephant to be sure, though when the need arises I believe I can give as good a buffet as any man. The two to whom I referred were Sir William and Sir Derek."

The poet started to chuckle. The chuckle changed to a laugh and then to paroxysms of laughter so that he slapped his thigh and fell to coughing until eventually he had to sit down on the side of the lake, still laughing.

"He has taken leave of his wits," said the Abbot.

"Not so," said the Irishman. "He but keeps pace with his wits while you lag behind yours.

"Plainly if I have been challenged by both Sir Derek and Sir William, and since I do not choose to flee, and since both challenges were issued within the same hour and for the same grave offense to their ladies, then both have an equal right to settle with me upon a field of honor. If one were given priority over the other, it would suggest that the latter held the honor of his lady less highly than the first and this would in itself be discourteous.

"Yet it would not be meet according to the rule of chivalry and knightly conduct for me to meet these two knights upon the field of honor at the same time.

"Therefore it is but just that Sir Derek and Sir William, to uphold the degree of esteem in which they hold their ladies, should first fight each other to see which of them should then have the right to meet me first. You have said yourself, my lord Abbot, that I am likely to be slain at the first encounter. That would leave the second knight without means of upholding the honor of his lady and avenging the slight against her imputed to me."

The Abbot now started to chuckle. The chuckle was visible first only in a slight shaking of the fat on his ample chest and belly, but soon this shaking had spread to his whole frame and, reaching his legs, sent widening rings of water out over the smooth surface of the lake.

"You are a nimble-witted rascal," he said, wiping his eyes. "The whole of Grand Fenwick has been waiting and planning for years to see these two bulls lock horns in the pasture. They go about bragging and rolling their muscles, each claiming himself the stronger and the braver and the more skillful. Yet their father has ever forbidden any contest between them and so they brag the louder, for I suspect they are glad of their father's ban which prevents the matter being put to the test.

"But now these two bulls, roaring and snorting at each other and pawing the ground, will be unleashed, and I suspect to their dismay. For it is my belief that Sir Derek fears Sir William as much as Sir William in secret fears Sir Derek. And they have been so nice about the honor of the Lady Matilda and Mistress Janice of Mountjoy that they cannot avoid the contest nor may their father, with any propriety, forbid it.

"Ah, it will be rich to see them trembling at the end of the lists, and awaiting the flourish of the heralds' trumpets signaling the charge."

"It seems to me," said Sir Dermot slyly, "that such an engagement—Gog against Magog as it were—should be preceded by some preliminary affairs, and a day of jousting should be arranged, with the principal event between Sir Derek and Sir William to cap the day's sport."

"You are a little behind the times," said the Abbot smoothly, "for this tournament has already been arranged and heralds are even now on their way to Italy, France and Switzerland to proclaim a Truce of God and invite the attendance of knights from these several countries at the tourney."

"You arranged a tournament thinking that I would flee?" asked

Sir Dermot.

"Sir Knight," said the Abbot, "it is my duty as the spiritual adviser of this blessed Duchy to inquire well into the character of all who visit this land so that I may protect my charges from them. As for your character, I know you as a roistering and worthless fellow, a pot-walloper and a hawk among the gentle doves of Christendom. In short even such a fellow as I was before repentance overtook me—perhaps a mite earlier than was necessary.

"Yet I have examined this armor of yours that you offer for sale and find it has sustained many blows and withstood much usage in war. So I did not think you would flee, though I hoped you would, for I have a liking for such damnable rogues as you. Rather I thought you would accept battle, and being shriven before entering the lists, would be dispatched to Heaven's gates, which would ease my conscience in respect of your immortal soul.

"I had not thought for this turn of events—this reversing of the table, so that Sir William must fight Sir Derek. You are more quick in your mind that I took you for.

"And yet perhaps you intend to grace the lists and may have your neck broken and so gain Heaven, being first shriven by myself?"

"Alas no, my lord Abbot," said Sir Dermot sadly. "It would not become me knightly honor to risk a neck which is forfeit either to Sir William or Sir Derek—whoever is the victor in their encounter. Added to which were I beaten to the ground and asked to yield, I would have nothing wherewith to ransom meself, being Irish and landless."

"It is the landless part of you that troubles me the most," said the Abbot. "But let me warn you—do not make any calves' eyes during your stay here, which I trust will be brief, at the Lady Matilda, or I will wring your neck."

"Have no fear about that," said the Irishman. "When this tournament is over and the matter of Sir William or Sir Derek is settled, whichever of the two I am to fight, I will go to Florence; for I am wiser than you think and see no reason why a man should content himself with one love when there are a score awaiting him in every town of the world."

The Abbot reeled in his line and sighed. "You are ripe for the Lord's harvest," he said. "And I must see to your reaping for I cannot let so spirited a man plunge onward to damnation."

CHAPTER VIII

CHARLES VII of France, nicknamed the "Well-Served" for reasons which were not always obvious to him, held a council of his advisers in Paris one month after the Battle of Formigny. The King sat not upon a throne, but upon a backless chair with an embroidered woolsack upon it, and around him were a number of low tables with bowls of fruit and sweetmeats. He picked cautiously at these, occasionally giving one to his mistress, Agnes Sorel, well advanced in her fourth pregnancy, or to one of the counselors in the room with him. For Charles, the Well-Served, lived in fear of being poisoned by his son, the Dauphin, or a score of other enemies who were in open or secret rebellion against him. He liked to be sure that others ate whatever he was eating.

He was not a striking figure of a man, this king who owed his crown to a peasant girl, Joan of Arc. He was weak of body and weak of mind and the prey of a thousand suspicions. To offset the shortcomings of his physique, his sky-blue undertunic, decorated with the lilies of France, was heavily padded at the shoulders and his thin arms were half concealed in bag sleeves of his outer garment of crimson.

His hose were padded down the calves and sometimes the padding got out of place and made it look as though he had a huge bump on the side of his leg. His eyes were a pale blue and his mouth a thin pink line and he had a crucifix of gold, set with rubies, dangling on his chest, for he had become somewhat religious in his middle years and had but recently advised the Pope that Joan of Arc should be canonized.

With the King were his brother-in-law, Charles of Anjou; Dunois, the energetic Bastard of Orleans; the King's brother, Arthur of Brittany, better known as the Comte de Richemont, victor of Formigny, and Constable of France, and Pierre de Brézé. The topic was what should be done now that the King's cannon had swept the English from the field at Formigny so that Calais was the only city in northern France which remained in the hands of England.

"Sire," said the Comte de Richemont, "we must next take Calais itself. Our cannon can breach the walls, and while the English retain one port in France, they threaten the whole of France."

"Calais is like a plum upon a tree whose roots have been cut," said the Bastard of Orleans. "The fruit will drop in time without our plucking it. It would be better, Sire, if we turned now to the southwest, to Guienne and Gascony where the English still hold power and where our rebellious French nobles still toast the King of England and proclaim themselves Gascons rather than Frenchmen."

"Nay, Sire," said Pierre de Brézé. "For a hundred years we have fought the English and now they are no longer our foremost enemies. They have troubles of their own in their wretched damp land, and what is true of Calais is true of Guienne and Gascony. These too are cut off from their roots and will in time fall to us.

"The true enemy lies in Dauphiné on the Swiss border, where Your Highness's own son, the Dauphin, rules over as big a mass of rascals as ever threatened the sovereignty and unity of France. It is there we should strike, Sire, for if your own son rebels against you and goes scatheless, it is a gross encouragement to others to defy your authority."

The King surveyed his advisers with his pale blue eyes and fingered the crucifix nervously and then looked at his mistress. It is possible that in that moment he reflected how much he owed to women—to the witch, soon to be made a saint, who had put him on the throne, and to the handsome and unofficial wife who now sat beside him, and going back a little farther, to his mother-in-law, Yolande of Aragon, who had rid him of his bad counselors in his early years—a task he had been incapable of performing himself. He instinctively distrusted the advice of men because he thought all men in giving him advice were bullying him. But women's advice he could take, for he never felt in it any challenge to his authority.

"What do you say, *petite*?" he asked of his mistress.

"Calais, Dauphiné, Guienne, Burgundy and Gascony," said Agnes Sorel, ticking them off on her fingers, "and there is one more which your advisers have overlooked."

"And what is that?" asked Dunois boldly.

"Grand Fenwick," replied Agnes Sorel.

At the mention of the name the King's round pale face flushed to a shrimp pink. He let go of the crucifix and put his hand with sudden fierce gesture to the jeweled hilt of a dagger which hung at his waist. He got up with a sudden clumsy movement, knocking a bowl of oranges to the floor. And then he kicked at the oranges, sending them scurrying across the floor of the council chamber.

"Grand Fenwick!" he spluttered. "Grand Fenwick! This little pimple of a place, tucked in the Alps, that has twice defied all the power of France and twice sent reeling back the armies dispatched to annihilate it. None, not even the English, have humbled us as much as this puppet principality. Do not talk to me of the Dauphin's rebellion. Who would not rebel against a king so ill-served that a handful of bastard Englishmen with one castle to their name can defy the whole power of France?

"No, my lords. The Lady Agnes is right. Not Dauphiné nor Calais, not Burgundy, Guienne nor Gascony but Grand Fenwick. There is the wellspring of revolt. There is the whole seedbed of impertinent insurrection against the throne of France. Crush Grand Fenwick if you seek to serve me. Destroy it. Annihilate it. Stamp it out. For if such a molehill can make a mock of France, then any cutthroat in my kingdom, any spoiled knight or demitered bishop can rise against me.

"I will have no authority over France while Grand Fenwick still exists independent. Therefore, Dunois, and you Pierre de Brézé, and you Richemont, Constable of France, collect between you such an army as has never marched before.

"Let there be knights and archers, spearmen and swordsmen. And let there be cannon. I care not if you take every piece of ordnance in France. But reduce this Grand Fenwick to ruins and bring me here the so-called Duke of this place in chains and tied to the tail of a cart. Then will I know that I am King of France and rule my lands."

And with that he kicked and stamped again at the oranges, squashing them to the floor and booting the flattened pulp across the room. And having done this he gave his arm to the Lady Agnes and escorted her from the council chamber, the padding in his hose much displaced by his paroxysm.

When the King had left, Dunois looked at Richemont the Constable, and Richemont shrugged. "Little kings pick themselves little wars," snorted Dunois.

"From what I know of Grand Fenwick," said Richemont, "this is likely to be no little war."

"Bah," snorted Dunois, "when the Maid and I routed the English at Orleans there was a battle worthy of the courage of France. But this Grand Fenwick! Oh that I should have lived to pit myself against such a pigmy."

"You fared better than the Maid, at that," said Richemont. "His Highness handed her over to her executioners—though he is to make a saint of her now. You are still alive. To have been the comrade in arms of a saint—that should be something, Dunois. I would say your place in Heaven is assured."

"If I gain Heaven," said Dunois, "it will be because there has been a great change in the rules of admission. Have we anywhere a map of this place Grand Fenwick? I only know vaguely where it is."

"It lies on the northern borders of Dauphiné, encompassed by the Alps," said the Constable. "Three days' march from Grand Fenwick to the west would take you to Guienne," he added slyly.

The point was not lost on Dunois. He smiled. "I have the King's authority to take with me the greatest army ever raised in France, my lord Constable," he said. "I will take this Grand Fenwick on a Monday between tierce and vespers and be in Guienne by the end of the week."

The great tournament of Grand Fenwick was held in the third week in June, under skies of luminous blue, and amid a countryside bright with wild rose and the flowers of the plum, hawthorn, cherry and apple, for Grand Fenwick, being situated in the Alps, had a late flowering of its fruit trees.

Sir Roger threw himself most heartily into the affair, with the assistance of the Lady Matilda. It was the Lady Matilda who supplied the tournament with a name. Since Sir Derek of Azule was her champion, and she fair-haired, and Sir William the Lady Janice's champion, and she dark-haired, she gave to the tournament the title of "The Conflict of the Knight Or and the Knight Sable" and requested that the two champions should paint their armor in these colors, and Sir William should wear a plume of black in his casque and a cape of black, while Sir Derek wore a golden plume and a golden cape.

These two hues were also used for the decorations of the pavilion from which the nobility would watch the tournament. The pavilion was built in a large meadow of perhaps a hundred acres within arrow flight of the castle and town of Grand Fenwick. It was draped gaily with banners and crowned with the arms of Grand Fenwick—a double-headed eagle saying "Aye" from one beak and "Nay" from the other, summarizing the greater part of the knowledge which the founder of the duchy had obtained at Oxford University.

Around the pavilion, itself decorated in black and gold, with many pennons, bannerols and bannerets flying from the roof, was the area for the tents of the knights taking part, or hoping to take part in the tourney. These were as gay as midsummer; some being of blue silk, others pink and black, others pale gold and others deep green and red and yet others particolored or striped. Outside of his tent each knight hung his shield upon a pole so that any who wished might ride by and strike it to signify a challenge given, and the day before the tournament there was many a merry ring as French, Italian and Swiss knights slapped their broadswords against these shields.

Behind the tents and the pavilion had been erected the booths of armorers and swordsmiths, blacksmiths and leeches and horse doctors and others whose presence was essential to the affair. And among these were the booths of the money-lenders ready to advance, at 8 percent compound interest, the crowns, florins, guilders, lire or reals which a knight might need either to pay his ransom or repair his armor or buy a horse or a spear or a shield, or even have his coat of arms repainted if it did not appear fresh enough to him.

The first to arrive in Grand Fenwick were this sort of people—the artisans of the tournaments; and they brought with them a number of wanton women who strode about, some of them in men's clothing, issuing challenges of their own which the good wives of Grand Fenwick were anxious to see that their men did not take up.

Next came the squires and heralds and the knights and in many cases their ladies, so that the castle, which often seemed to the Lady Matilda so empty, was now full of a diverse number of people, gaily dressed, gaily spoken, given to the song and the dance, and the women full of notes upon houppelands, cotehardies, hennins and mantles and the various materials out of which these might be contrived.

With all these people the Lady Matilda noted that Sir Dermot mixed freely and on the easiest and friendliest terms, being able to talk their differing languages, and popular because of this and because of his witty tongue and ability with the lute. It was he who, when conversation lagged in the Red Hall, or around the now crowded table of Sir Roger in the Great Hall, revived it with a quip or a snatch of verse or a tale of romance. This, plus the fact that Sir Dermot seemed determined never to be alone in her company, annoyed the Lady Matilda and she discussed it with her constant companion, the Lady Janice.

"I have a feeling," she said, "that he is afraid of me. A look comes into his eyes, whenever I contrive to find him solitary, which seems close to panic. Yet when others are present, he is merry and provocative and, I fancy, looks at me with desire."

"He is in love but fears love," said the Lady Janice, who was shrewd in these matters.

"Oh, how romantic," sighed the Lady Matilda. "Do you suppose he once loved a maiden of much higher degree than himself, and saw her slain before his eyes because she would not marry another?"

"You mistake the man for the tales he tells," said the Lady Janice. "I think he is merely afraid of being married. He is one who wants all the pleasure of love but none of the dullness."

"Love could never be dull," said the Lady Matilda, dreamily. "It is an enchantment, full of pleasure and pain, of fulfillment and loneliness, of hope and anguish. It is like the small stream in the mountain which rushes hungrily and anxiously down to the sea, filled with hope and desire to be lost in the great body of the water, yet filled also with fear that on the way its path may be dammed and it will never reach its love.

"Or it is like the young grass at night, newborn and dependent for its life upon the rising of the sun, waiting with anxiety and hope for the staining of the eastern skies with light, and yet fearful that the shadows of night will never go and the sun will never rise…"

"Or," said Sir Dermot, who had come up unseen, "it is like a harp new-made but unplayed, waiting for the fingers which will give it voice, but fearful that they will play upon another; or a ship, long at anchor, which hears the call of the wind and the tide and longs for the great ocean but cannot break free; or it is like rain long held in the loneliness of the skies and longing for the soft bosom of the earth…"

"Sir Dermot," said the Lady Matilda. "You must have known much love to speak so sweetly and readily of it."

"Oh," said Sir Dermot, "'tis a living in a manner of speaking. Few things are more highly recompensed than a tale of romance."

"And yet," said the Lady Matilda, "I think you long for some love from whom you are separated by a cruel fate. Perhaps your lady in Ireland whom you have not seen in many years, for I am told you are married…"

"Heaven forbid," said Sir Dermot with a shudder, "matrimony is one of the few perils I have escaped. Like death it disagrees violently with me life."

"Ah, Sir Dermot," said the Lady Matilda, "would it not be wondrous to spend every day of your life blessed by the presence of your beloved; to have the earth made sweeter, the sun warmer, by the knowledge that she was there?"

"It would not," said the knight, "for I have known a great quantity of married knights and others of higher degree, and all of them forever chasing stags or boars or wolves or Frenchmen or Saracens or whatever there is to chase to be away from their ladies. It comes to me mind that matrimony is a great slayer of stags and popularizer of horses. For a man may yearn for his lady love all his life but for his wife he will not yearn more than three months before he is on his horse and away from her."

"You speak harshly of marriage," chided the Lady Matilda.

"It is a dungeon into which a man may be thrown in his prime and from which he can expect no ransom," said Sir Dermot. "Therefore either he becomes resigned to his state, which is to say he becomes resigned to the loss of freedom, or he rebels against it, and in the very rebelling acknowledges that his freedom has gone and he a full man no more.

"In either case his condition is pitiable. But I have so far, as I say, escaped the peril."

"And have you never loved?" asked the Lady Matilda.

"It was my habit to fall in love six times in the year," said Sir Dermot. "But knowing myself fickle I took none of these sieges seriously. Now, being older, I fall in love but twice in the year."

"…and this year?" prompted the Lady Matilda.

"The year is yet early," said Sir Dermot. "But let us join the others in the courtyard, for I learn that a game of tennis is to be played by one of the French against one of the Italians, both players being highly skilled."

The Lady Matilda sighed. All her conversations with Sir Dermot ended thus—with an invitation to be among others. She wished she had the will power to refuse to accompany the Irishman, but being in his presence gave her a kind of anguished pleasure, while being absent from him filled her with longing and melancholy.

CHAPTER IX

THE two knights of Azule, Sir William and Sir Derek, were the only ones in the Duchy of Grand Fenwick who took no pleasure at all in the prospect of the tournament. They had been informed that they were to be pitted against each other by Sir Roger himself and the matter filled them with misgiving. Each went separately to his father, the Count of Azule, and pleaded that he did not wish to kill his brother, and the Count went to Sir Roger and said it would be a hard thing if he lost one or both of his sons in a tournament because of a confounded outlander who, if the truth were plainly spoken, was too cowardly to fight.

"I agree with you on the Irishman," said Sir Roger. "I think his courage is all in his mouth. But I have lately come to suspect something of the sort also concerning your twin sons."

"Your Grace," said the Count, "you offer me an insult."

"Perhaps," said Sir Roger. "But these two champions of yours have stamped and bellowed so long, protesting how the one could best the other if you did not forbid it, that it is only right the matter should be put to the test. Furthermore I need to know the true character of all of my subjects who may one day bear arms in the cause of their country. Do not fear to lose them. If they do not fight they will be lost in manhood to you in any case. And if they do, I fancy they will be so anxious to avoid each other's blows that hardly a rivet will be started in their armor."

"I will warrant they will fight as good, aye, better than any man," said the Count shortly. He, therefore, returned to his sons, berated them for seeking to avoid the encounter, and threatened that he would cut either or both of them off from their inheritance if they showed cowardice in the lists.

Thereafter the two brothers practiced and exercised with the weapons separately, fearful that some special skill or technique developed should be discovered by the other. Breakspear, who had long smarted under them because they reviled him as a clerk, sought his revenge by filling each full of fears by reporting on the other's proficiency and hours of practice.

"I have the two of them practicing three hours a day with the broadsword, two with the mace and spiked ball, and two with the lance," he told the Abbot Almin. "I believe I can increase this so that they spend ten hours a day sweating in their armor."

"You will have them worn out before the tournament," cautioned the Abbot.

"Sir William now carries a spear of eighty pounds," continued Breakspear, "and next week it will be one of eighty-five, for I will tell him that is the weight of the spear adopted by his brother."

"No man may hold such a spear before him," said the Abbot.

"They are to fight in the French style," said the poet. "A mounted squire will go before each of them with the end of the spear resting upon his shoulder. Then a few moments before the impact, the squires will pull their palfreys aside, and our two knights have but to hold these young trees level for a second or two for the onslaught to take place."

"And who will these squires be?" asked the Abbot.

"That is not yet agreed upon," replied the poet.

"But whoever they are, they must have more hardihood than our two knights."

After this conversation the Abbot summoned Sir Derek to him and the knight arrived red-faced, sweating and nervous.

"I hear that you will fight after the manner of the French," said the Abbot. "That is, your lances will be supported until a few moments before the impact, on the shoulders of squires?"

"That is so," said Sir Derek.

"Then let me recommend you a good squire for your service," said the Abbot. "Never mind about the reputation he sets upon himself. It is but his modesty. But you will find no better man than the poet, Nicholas Breakspear."

"Breakspear!" snorted Sir Derek. "He is but a bookman and has the heart of a sick chicken."

"Tush," said the Abbot. "One should not judge by public reputation. That is but what he says of himself, for he does not want to be known by his true merits. The fellow is in fact a veritable Alexander. I hear that he has himself offered Sir Dermot a buffet for the honor—er—of Grand Fenwick. If you take my advice you will lay public claim to his service by posting notice that he is your choice as squire for the tournament. He may then not refuse you without payment of a forfeit of a hundred crowns which I know he has not got.

"And while we are thus talking, I commend your daily exercise with arms. Yet with such a dread event before you, my son, would it not be wise to be equally diligent in your spiritual exercises and attend to the worship of God regularly each day now, both in the morning services and the evening services?"

"I agree that it would," said Sir Derek soberly.

"Then do not fail to be in the Virgin's Chapel this evening," said the Abbot and dismissed him.

He then sent for the other brother and recommended to him as his squire a young groom, who was negligent often in his church attendance, and also charged Sir William that since death might be his fate in a matter of days, he should also attend more strictly to his worship of God.

Within the hour Breakspear burst in upon the Abbot. He was highly excited; his eyes bright with fear.

"What evil have I done you that you send me to my death, carrying upon my shoulder the lance head of that oaf Sir Derek, with his brother's lance aimed at my chest?" he demanded.

"Why none at all," said the Abbot cheerfully. "I look only to your spiritual welfare. You will find, my son, that Mother Church, in her love for her children, never ceases to plan and to pray that they will attend more zealously to their religious exercises. You will hardly refrain, now that you are to enter the lists with, as you say, a lance on your shoulder and another pointed at your chest, from coming more frequently to church, though you have sneered at these duties in the past, to the peril of your soul."

"I believe," stormed the poet, "you would kill a man to get him to Heaven."

"None enter without dying," said the Abbot casually. "It is the accepted thing. You will be at Benediction this evening?"

"Yes," snarled the poet.

A little later came the groom, who upon being reminded also of the perils which lay ahead, agreed readily to attend divine services twice a day until the tournament.

"This has been a blessed day," said the Abbot when he went to bed that night. "I have labored well in the vineyards and brought four souls nearer to the Grace of God. But I will not rest until I have that Irish rogue upon his knees before me."

It was not only the Abbot who was laying snares for the Irishman but the Lady Matilda also. She asked the Lady Janice for advice how best to trap him—though she did not put it in that manner.

"Well," said Janice, who was of a practical nature, "you could fall sick and ask that he come and play the lute to you in your chamber—with me in attendance, of course. And then I could wander off and leave you two alone…"

"Oh, no," said the Lady Matilda, blushing. "I could never do that."

"Why?" asked Janice coolly.

"Because…because he has such a roguish look to him. I wouldn't trust him in my bedchamber alone with me."

"Is that so?" said Janice thoughtfully. "How interesting. I hadn't thought of it. Well, then, I will fall sick and…"

"Oh, no, you don't," said the Lady Matilda. "I don't trust you either."

"My dear," said Janice, "to trap a man you must either compromise him or make him jealous. You'll never make that Irish fox jealous. So you must compromise him. If he were found alone in your bedchamber by your father, the Duke, you'd be wed in a day."

"You don't know my father," said Matilda. "He'd pitch him through the window forty feet to the courtyard below. That wouldn't work at all. I was thinking, perhaps, something romantic could be arranged—like a rescue."

"Rescue, indeed," said Janice. "Unless I am utterly wrong, that worthless knight has never rescued anything but the money he was forced to put into a collection plate and for which he no doubt later robbed the poor box. Don't go putting yourself in peril and expecting him to save you. He'd feed you to a dragon to save his own skin."

"Ah, you misjudge him cruelly," said Matilda. "He is wicked, I know. But he is good really. And he seems cowardly, yet I know him to be brave."

"Well," said Janice, "if you stake your life on it, you will lose your life."

"What is life without my love?" said the Lady Matilda woefully.

"It's boring at times," admitted Janice, "but there's always dinner to be looked forward to."

"I am sure he loves me," said Matilda. "I believe you are right when you say that he loves me but fears to admit it."

"I didn't know that I ever said that," replied Janice. "But the fear part of it is true. He is so full of fear that he would not even accept the challenges of Sir William and Sir Derek, but made them fight each other. Though it serves them right. I'm sick of their posturings."

"One day he will save me from a dire peril," said Matilda.

"One day he will let you break your pretty little neck trying to prove that," replied her companion.

CHAPTER X

THE tournament commenced with a great parade of the Knights Sable and the Knights Or around the field and past the pavilion in which the Ladies Matilda and Janice reigned as joint queens of the event. All the knights who were to take part had chosen either gold or black as trimming for their horses and their armor in honor of one or the other of these two ladies and they made a most noble sight as they walked, six paces ahead of their horses, which were led by their squires or pages.

Each knight, in addition to the trimmings of black or gold, wore a surcoat displaying his arms on front and back, and the display of colors and designs and charges was exciting and impressive. Sir Ferdinand of Berne, a short, stocky Swiss knight, bore three luces azure quartered on a field argent; Sir Tome of Castel de Madre de Dios from Italy, a tall thin Italian, bore a wyvern gules on a field or; Sir François de Chateaunoir, a leopard sable, rampant et regardant, on a field gules.

This noble procession of knights was led across the lists by Sir Roger of Grand Fenwick, his sturdy, blocky figure clad in armor with over it the surcoat displaying the charge of his dukedom—a double-headed eagle, gules, on a field argent. A squire walked before Sir Roger carrying the Duke's broadsword inherited from his grandfather and called the Wing of Death. This sword had a blade four feet long and a pommel of a foot in length, so that the total length of the weapon was some five feet. It was a weapon somewhat out of fashion, but it was the one with which Sir Roger would fight, and as the people of the Duchy saw their Duke approaching the pavilion at the head of the procession, there to do his honor to his daughter and the Lady Janice, joint queens of the tournament, they raised a cheer for him, for they loved him to a man.

Behind Sir Roger came the knight whom he had challenged—the Count of Chaux de Fonds, a dark-haired, swarthy man, several inches taller than Sir Roger. His page carried before him his weapon—a heavy battle-ax. Looking at these weapons, the people around got confirmation of a rumor which had been current for some days—that Sir Roger and the Count were to fight to the death or until one of them would yield his life for ransom.

Each knight, arriving before the center of the pavilion where the two queens of the tournament were enthroned, stopped, bowed and commended his service to his particular lady, and then leaped upon his horse, and crying his battle cry, galloped off to his tent to arm himself for the foray.

All this made the Ladies Matilda and Janice very happy, and

they blushed prettily and bowed their heads most graciously as each knight presented himself, his title being announced by the heralds.

It also made Sir Dermot of Ballycastle very happy.

Sir Dermot was seated between the two ladies, though how he got to be there nobody seemed quite to know. And he was holding the left hand of the Lady Matilda and the right hand of the Lady Janice, having explained to them that he wished to show favor neither to one nor the other lest he receive several more challenges from others of their champions.

When Sir Derek, who for the purposes of the tournament was given the title of the Lone Knight Or, was presented before the pavilion and saw Sir Dermot holding the hand of the Lady Matilda he so far forgot his courtesy as to shake his fist at the Irishman. And when Sir William, the Lone Knight Sable of the tournament, was likewise presented he had to be restrained by the heralds from climbing into the pavilion and engaging Sir Dermot there and then.

But Sir Dermot was not a whit perturbed. He smiled at the fuming knights and whispered in the ear of the Lady Matilda or the Lady Janice, bringing his lips very close to their cheeks, which did nothing to improve the disposition of the Lone Knight Sable or the Lone Knight Or.

The forenoon of the tournament was taken up with the preliminary bouts between various knights. Sir Tome of Castel de Madre de Dios was unhorsed by a knight from Germany who flung him out of his saddle after but three passes. Sir Guillaume of Milan beat Sir François de Chateau-noir to his knees after but forty minutes of thwacking at each other afoot with the broadsword. Sir Ferdinand of Berne was the winner of an uncontested event, his opponent having been overtaken by an attack of hiccups when fully armored and rendered incapable of taking the field. These events were watched with a polite interest rather than great excitement. There was, in fact, a certain amount of impatience among the spectators, for all were looking forward to the two main events of the tourney, the collision between the two Goliaths—the Lone Knight Sable and the Lone Knight Or—and the battle between Sir Roger and the Count of Chaux de Fonds.

In the tents of the two knights of Azule, meanwhile, some very unknightly scenes were taking place. Nicholas Breakspear, having had his fortieth resignation from the position of squire rejected by Sir Derek, had disappeared for the third time and been discovered among the crowd disguised as a woman. He had now been brought back and put under guard lest he try to escape again. He sat upon a stool wringing his hands, at a loss for further argument or plan with which to save his life, for he was sure it was forfeit.

Sir Derek was in no better condition and in his own anxiety paid little attention to the sufferings of his squire. He had armored himself twice and had twice had the armor removed, for he was sweating so much that it became unbearable. He had sent for the Abbot and been shriven, and had then sent for the Abbot once more to be shriven again, having recalled several matters which had escaped him at his previous confession.

His father, the Count of Azule, came to his tent and, finding his son so distraught, spoke roundly to him and hastened off to the tent of his other son, Sir William. Here he was unfortunate enough to overhear Sir William offering a blacksmith a hundred crowns to don his armor and fight in his stead.

"By Our Lady," cried the Count, "it seems that Sir Roger was right and you are craven after all."

"Nay, Sire," said Sir William, swiftly regaining his wits, "it is only that I know my own prowess and fear that I may kill my brother. Ask my page, the groom there."

"Well, boy?" asked the Count. "How is it? How does he behave?"

"Most piously," said the groom. "He has spent so much time upon his knees with Pater Nosters and Aves that I cannot get his greaves on him. Having heard that Sir Derek his brother was twice shriven, he has himself been shriven thrice, and the Abbot Almin has sworn that he is worn out with absolution and will shrive him no more. It seems to me that the contest between the two is who shall be in the greater state of grace when he dies."

"Do not mention death," snapped Sir William. "It is bad luck."

"You are not afraid, boy?" asked the Count.

"No, my lord," said the groom. "I was afraid until I saw Sir William and then my fears left me."

"Hah," said the Count proudly, "his courage and bearing have driven out your fears."

"No," said the groom. "It was rather the opposite."

"How do you mean?" demanded the Count.

"Why," replied the groom, "I found your son trembling upon his knees and the tent being small can contain only a certain amount of fear and so mine was driven out."

"Ah then," said the Count, "it is true and my son is afraid."

"He says it is because he does not wish to kill his brother," replied the groom. "And who are we to say he lies, for a man newly shriven will hardly lie in the face of death."

"Don't say 'death,'" thundered Sir William. "I have warned you it is bad luck."

"Sir Knight," said the groom, "it is I who will ride before you with your spear head upon my shoulder and it is I who am likely to be the first spitted. Therefore if the word 'death' brings bad luck it is likely to bring it more to me than to you. Yet I will say 'death' and 'death' again and it pleases me. And now, Sir Knight, if you will give me your foot, I will get your sollerets fitted though the toes cannot be put on until you are mounted, since they are too long and pointed for you to walk about in."

"These elbow cops are so stiff I cannot bend my arm," Sir William grumbled.

"If they are stiff, they will help you support your lance when I am gone from under it, which will be as speedily as possible," said the groom.

"You are to support the lance until the white line is reached," said Sir William warmly. "Otherwise I will wring your neck."

"If I am gone from under it too quickly," said the squire, "your lance head will drop to the ground and shock your arm and hand so rudely that you will not be able to wring the neck of as much as a chicken for three months. Come, give me your foot."

"You talk rudely to your knight," said the Count of Azule. "When I was a young man, such things were unheard of."

"Aye, my lord," replied the groom, "and likely when you were a young man squires were not called upon to battle beside knights in the lists. I never swore to defend the Lady Janice nor ever touched her ankle."

"You talk like a churl," said the Count. "You show your base blood and will never be a knight though you play the part of a squire, and that poorly."

"That is no loss," said the groom. For if Sir Dermot is to be credited, then when I am grown, knights will be out of date and armor useless. He has offered me his for five crowns, but I have no need of it. Nor have I five crowns."

"The blackguardly rascal," snorted the Count. "Offering to sell his armor to a groom. My son," he continued, turning toward Sir William, "I will myself engage Sir Dermot if today's encounter on the field of honor should result in your death."

"Don't say 'death,'" said Sir William. "I beg of you don't say 'death.'"

His father blessed him and left, first warning him that if he as much as flinched upon the field, he would forfeit his inheritance.

"Do not be downcast, Sir William," said the groom. "You may flinch in your armor like an oyster under the juice of limes but none will see you. And that charger of yours, the Thunderer of Flanders, has such an iron mouth that you could not turn him aside, once started, if you had ten times your strength. Touch him with the spur and he will show enough courage for the two of you and likely will not stop until he is in France. It was yourself that trained him."

"I trained him for the battle charge, not the lists," said Sir William sulkily.

"The lists are a battle, for many die in them," said the groom.

"If you mention 'death' again," said William screaming, "I will brain you with my gauntlet."

At last the time arrived for the combat between the two.

The Herald Sable and the Herald Or walked in their tabards to the center of the field, and faced the pavilion. The heralds announced that no quarrel lay between the two knights but that they fought to settle a point of honor in keeping with the noblest spirit of knightly courtesy. This point of honor consisted in deciding which of them should have the right to first engage Sir Dermot of Ballycastle in a fight to the death for having offered a slight to their ladies. The heralds announced that the slight offered to the two ladies, who were queens of the tournament, had been offered on the same hour and on the same day and was of the same degree. This brought a series of whistles and hurrahs from the churls and serfs and peasants on the far side of the field, and many of the knights in the pavilion (their ladies too) strained to catch a better glimpse of the Irishman who, they decided, must be a lover of the persuasiveness of Galahad. Sir Dermot rose with a display of modesty and bowed to all and sat down again.

When the heralds had finished their announcement, they retired to the side of the lists. Trumpeters then raised their long instruments and, accompanied by a roll on the kettledrums, sounded a fanfare and Nicholas Breakspear, squire of Sir Derek, the Knight Or, appeared on one side of the list, mounted on a jennet. Those close enough to the poet were surprised to see that he was roped to the saddle. He held between his hands a small piece of earthenware jar, and the Abbot Almin, who was with him, was shaking with laughter and endeavoring to assure the poet that what he held was a shard of the pot from which the saintly Andreas of Antioch had slaked his thirst after forty years of fasting in the deserts of Egypt.

Behind the poet was the black-armored figure of Sir Derek, mounted upon a dappled stallion. The stallion stood seventeen hands at the shoulders, but despite his huge size, it was dwarfed by the mountainous knight upon its back. He wore a casque of Italian design, pointed in the front like the bow of a ship, so that his huge armored head seemed like something seen in a nightmare. The cops or elbow pieces of his armor were spiked, and his sollerets or shoes had pointed toes eight inches long which could be put into place with a metal pin only when the knight was mounted.

At the same time his brother, Sir William, the Lone Knight Sable, appeared with his squire at the other end of the field. His helmet, of French design, was of the kind known as armet à roundelle—the skull part in one piece, the gorget protecting the neck another, and the ventail and visor, guarding the eyes and face, in a solid piece of fluted steel. The side view, since the casque was noseless, was remarkably like the profile of a gorilla. The knight's chest was protected by a plate of steel which came to a sharp ridge in the center, to throw off a spear thrust, and beneath the joints of the armor were pieces of chain mail, fixed to a leather shirt which the knight wore beneath his suit of steel. A slight tinkling sound, audible to the ears of the groom if to none other, suggested that the knight was trembling and the mail patches below his armor beating a little tattoo on the steel skin.

But when these two knights appeared at the opposite ends of the lists, gigantic and impressive, a sigh of wonder and apprehension went around the tournament spectators. They looked like two evil colossi, the one black, the other gold. They moved their heads and arms and legs slowly beneath the weight of their armor, and this gave to them a curious and frightening mechanical character. Their arms bearers lifted their big shields up to them and, in the silence, the clang and scrape of the shields as they were brought into place against the armor of the knights could be distinctly heard and caused the skin on many a scalp to creep.

Next came the spears, thirty feet in length and weighing eighty pounds. It took three men, mounting small stands, to lift these monstrous weapons up to each knight, and again a sigh went through the spectators. Each knight had upon the right side of his armor, close to his armpit, a hinge projecting out from the breastplate, into which a pin on the shaft of the spear fitted. This hinge served as a rest for the spear, locking it securely to the knight, for he could not bear the great weight of the butt in one arm. The after part of the spear, behind this hinge, was passed under the armpit and projected beyond the back of the knight. The front of the spear was then lifted onto the left shoulder of the squire, who rode about fifteen feet in front of his knight.

Toward the center of the field of combat, two strips of white linen had been pegged to the ground. These were fifteen feet apart. They marked the spot where each squire could pull his horse aside, leaving his knight to hold the spear level by his own weight and momentum until he was upon his opponent. If he could catch his opponent anywhere on the trunk with the spear, he would certainly unhorse him and in all probability kill him, for the impact would be enormous.

"I fear they will be slain," said the Lady Matilda with a slight shudder.

Sir Dermot's reply was lost in a fanfare of trumpets, and before this was finished, Sir Derek had spurred his big stallion forward and the jennet of his squire, Breakspear, fearful of being run down by the charger, sprang ahead itself. So the Knight Or charged upon the Knight Sable before the Knight Sable was ready for him. But Sir William, seeing his peril, spurred the Thunderer of Flanders, and, better served by his squire, started toward his brother.

The distance across the lists was about five hundred yards. The four horsemen converged on each other to a thundering of hoofs which shook the ground around. The plumes of the knights streamed behind them, and their chargers, entering into the spirit of the contest, extended their tails and neighed their defiance the one of the other.

Breakspear, upon his jennet, was in a black panic. Before him, he could see looming larger and larger the monstrous black-clad Sir William. Or, to be more accurate, he could see the head of Sir William's lance, like a pointed battering ram, coming closer and closer and always pointing directly at his chest. He had, in his fear, forgotten about the white line and when he remembered it, he could not recall whether he had passed it or not, and dared not take his eyes off the lance tip plunging toward him.

"Blessed Saint Luke," he cried, recalling in his anguish the only one of the Apostles credited with a literary style, "protect me now." In the same moment he jerked the head of his jennet over to the right, ducking out from underneath the lance of his knight, which up to that moment he had held upon his shoulder. The poet had pulled away too soon, and Sir Derek's charger was flying at full gallop. Sir Derek tried manfully to keep the end of his lance up in the air, for there were still fifty yards to go before the impact. But it was useless. Slowly the lance point lowered to the ground as Sir Derek rose in his saddle and tried by his weight to bring it up. He wanted to throw the lance away and pull his charger off to the side. But the lance was fixed to his armor and his charger had a mouth of iron and had entered into the game with the fullest zest and energy. The stallion increased its stride. Sir Derek gave up the struggle and his lance point plunged suddenly to the ground.

What happened next astonished all. Sir Derek was in a second flipped out of his saddle like a pole jumper. Up he went into the air in a swift and graceful arc, slowing a little as he reached the apex of a huge semicircle which he was describing. It seemed for a moment that he had stopped his ascent and would come down on the same side as he had risen. But he continued, after hesitating a fraction of a second in mid-air, over the apex of the arc and started down the other side with increasing velocity.

Sir William's squire, meantime, being a lad of quick wits, took his cue from Breakspear. He also jerked from underneath his knight's lance, leaving Sir William to battle with the enormous lever of which his breastplate was the fulcrum. Sir William, like his brother, struggled gamely for a few seconds but lost to the force of gravity, and his lance head also entered the ground.

He too was jerked from his saddle and flung up in the air on the end of his lance. But he did not travel as far as Sir Derek. Indeed, he was on his way up when he encountered, in mid-air, his brother who was on his way down. The two met, perhaps seventeen feet above the ground, with a clang like ten blacksmiths striking ten anvils. Then they fell their separate ways to the turf below.

When the heralds got to them, they were both unconscious, and a shout went up that the squires should be hung. But Sir Roger, presiding at a court of arms which was summoned immediately, ruled that to hang the squires would merely discourage others from serving in that capacity.

An attempt was made by the Count of Azule to argue that since Sir Derek has passed the apex of his arc before the mid-air collision took place, he should be counted the winner, but Sir Roger would not have it that way, since both knights had been rendered hors de combat.

"They must fight again," said Sir Roger grimly. "Nothing has been settled here. They must meet once more or announce themselves satisfied and withdraw their challenge to Sir Dermot."

Sir Dermot went later in the day to visit the two champions in their beds. They lay in the same chamber, commiserating with each other, and glowered at the Irishman when he entered. Their father was with them, and bristled at the entry of the Irish knight.

"You are two foolish fellows," said Sir Dermot, ignoring the black looks. "The honor of a knight or of any man is not upheld by silly posturings and threats, by issuing challenges designed not to protect the weak but to prove the courage of the challenger.

"You have spent so many years asserting your merits that you have weakened whatever merits of manhood you possessed. Had I given you real offense, you had a right to challenge me. But in challenging me you were seeking only to prove yourselves brave and not to protect the honor of your ladies.

"If you still find yourselves offended, I will meet the first of you who can get himself out of bed. In the meantime, think over whether you behave like men or boys. For the basis of knighthood is manliness and not boyish posturing."

"Sir Dermot," said the Count of Azule, "I consider that in bringing about a spectacle which has made a laughingstock of my sons, you have done me grave injustice. And I do therefore challenge you in defense of the honor of my name."

"Old warrior," said the Irishman, "it is not I who have harmed your name but your two silly sons. They will no doubt make men yet, but it is your task to show them the road to manhood.

"If tomorrow when thinking over this, you still feel I have done you dishonor, then I will accept your challenge. But do not hold honor so shallow as to find it harmed when no harm exists."

With that Sir Dermot left. And on the morrow, having received no challenge from the Count of Azule, he assumed that the old knight had thought more fully on the matter and was directing his corrections and lessons in chivalry to Sir William and Sir Derek.

CHAPTER XI

IT WAS on the second day of the tournament, and in the afternoon, that the contest between Sir Roger of Grand Fenwick and Gridaud, Comte de Chaux de Fonds, took place. The morning was devoted to the archery contest, open to all, at which the prize was to be a purse of silver presented by Sir Roger.

Sir Roger originally had wished to limit this contest to the men of Grand Fenwick. It was the Abbot who persuaded him to open it to all comers.

"Let us show to all the superiority of our bowmen, my lord," he said. "It will be no bad thing to do since there will be many of the French watching."

In this light, Sir Roger then threw the contest open. But to the surprise of all it was won not by a man of Grand Fenwick nor one of the Genoese, who were reckoned good men with the bow, nor one of the Swiss, but by Sir Dermot of Ballycastle.

Sir Dermot made no bones over his reasons for entering the

contest. Unable to sell his armor—and he had made several endeavors to sell it to the knights visiting the tourney or to their more ambitious squires—he was still desperately short of money. And he told Sir Roger frankly when he put his name down among the lists of contestants that it was the purse of silver he was after.

This enraged Sir Roger even more against the Irish knight. He regarded it, in the first instance, as ungentlemanly for a knight to compete in a contest designed primarily for the Commons. And he regarded it as outrageous that even if a knight did so, he should announce so cheerfully that it was the money he was after.

"Bah, Sir Dermot," he snorted, "it has been truly said that the Irish are a beggarly nation."

"It has indeed," said Sir Dermot, "but it should be added that it was the English that beggared them. Of course, if you feel that I might outshoot your good men of Grand Fenwick, I will withdraw my entry."

"Outshoot them!" spluttered Sir Roger. "There's hardly a boy of eight in Grand Fenwick who could not outshoot you, and that without using half his skill."

But as matters developed, the Irishman showed an extraordinary skill with the longbow. Out of a field of three hundred in the first shoot, he was one of the hundred and twenty who survived. In the next shoot—three arrows at three hundred paces, the mark being a ball of parchment hung from a tree and swinging in the wind—he was one of the twenty who survived. Out of this twenty, at two hundred paces, but the mark being a hare released from a trap, he was one of the five who survived.

And out of this five, with but one arrow allowed to each archer and the mark a silver coin sent spinning in the air, he alone struck it with his arrow.

The performance had never been equaled in Grand Fenwick and Robin Goodspeed, Piers of the Glebe, Tom-a-Running and others of the freemen of Grand Fenwick who had competed against him, when they heard the clink of his arrow against the spinning coin, gave a roar of approval and seized the Irishman by his gangling legs and carried him on their shoulders around the field.

Even Sir Roger unbent sufficiently to ask him, while presenting the purse of silver coins, how he had come by his skill.

"Before I got the sword and spurs of knighthood," said Sir Dermot, "my life depended many a time on the longbow."

"You served in the wars as a bowman then?" said Sir Roger.

"I did," said Sir Dermot, "in between shooting for prizes at country fairs."

Sir Roger frowned and went off to his tent to arm himself for the combat. Sir Dermot, however, did not mount into the pavilion to seat himself between the Lady Matilda and the Lady Janice as he had done on the previous day. Instead he sought out the Abbot, whom he found among the common folk by the side of the tournament enclosure, his beads in one hand and a massive mace in the other.

"You carry the arms both spiritual and temporal today," said Sir Dermot eying the beads and the mace.

"I serve the Duke with both of them," said the Abbot,

smoothly. "With these"—showing the beads—"I beseech the Lord for his victory. And with this"—showing the mace—"I intend to knock the brains out of that damnable Frenchman if he take but the slightest unfair advantage of Sir Roger."

Sir Dermot noted that around the Abbot were some four or five hundred of the men of Grand Fenwick. They wore short swords and daggers. He looked across the lists and saw, at the other side, an equal number of Frenchmen, equally armed.

"I am told," he said, "that Gridaud of Chaux de Fonds practices daily with his battle-ax, and this is to be an engagement to the death."

"He has need of such practice," said the Abbot stoutly, "for I have known Sir Roger in battle to cleave a man through the chine as if he were a pastry."

Further conversation was interrupted by the heralds who advanced to the center of the lists and sounded a fanfare upon their trumpets. There were three heralds—one for the Frenchman, one for Sir Roger, and a third, handsomely tabarded in pure white and representing the Spirit of Chivalry. This last, when the fanfare had ceased, announced the combat between Roger, Duke of Grand Fenwick, and Gridaud, Count of Chaux de Fonds, with sharpened weapons to death or until one of them should yield.

Any who interfered with the combat, other than the heralds, he announced, would be summarily hung, and any who sought to give a weapon to one of the knights, should he become disarmed, would be handed over to the followers of the other knight to be done with as they wished.

Sir Roger, he announced, had elected to fight dismounted and without his shield. Sir Gridaud would fight mounted, but as a concession to his opponent would not armor his horse. These announcements completed, the heralds withdrew to the side of the lists, gave a further flourish on their trumpets, and the two contestants took the field.

Sir Roger entered first carrying his huge sword across his shoulder and looking neither to the right nor left. He was clad in chain mail—a style of armor which had all but gone out of fashion in favor of the heavier plate—and his casque was of the round can type with a flat top and bars over the face. It was armor which would have become a knight in the service of Simon de Montfort two hundred or more years previously, and there was a chuckle from the French when they caught sight of the short, blocky knight in his outdated suit of steel. Sir Roger paid no heed to this but walked or rather plodded to the center of the list, took his huge sword off his shoulder, with one hand whirled it over his head so that it became a circle of shimmering steel above him and sent out a deep hum, and then thrust it point down into the ground before him.

This done, he put his two hands on his hips and called aloud, "At your service, Gridaud of Chaux de Fonds."

"And yours, Sir Roger," cried Sir Gridaud and entered the list on his charger, clad cap-a-pie in black plate armor and holding in his right hand, the head almost touching the ground, a double-bitted battle-ax. In the silence that followed all that could be heard was the muffled thumping of the charger's hoofs as it went in a short gallop into the arena. When he was well into the combat area, Sir Gridaud reined in his charger and closed his visor which had been opened up to that time, and the slight clink it made as it shut had an air of grim finality to it which drew a sigh from the men of Grand Fenwick. Then, still trailing his battle-ax, he rode at a short gallop around the outer perimeter of the lists, his charger stirring up a cloud of dust, and returned to rein in before the pavilion. Here he bowed in the saddle to the two ashen-faced queens of the tournament, turned his horse's head slowly away toward Sir Roger, still standing in the center, and slowly raised his battle-ax across the pommel of his saddle and then, driving an inch of rowel into the flanks of his charger, drove down upon the lone mailclad figure which awaited him.

He sped past Sir Roger so swiftly that few saw precisely what happened. They caught a glimpse of the battle-ax raised, of Sir Gridaud standing in his stirrups, of the arc of the ax as it swung down in the sun like a hawk, and then for a second Sir Roger was hidden from them by the cloud of dust from the horse's hoofs. When the dust settled it was seen that Sir Roger was no longer standing, but was down upon one knee.

"Impossible!" cried the Abbot, staring in disbelief.

He had no time to say more for Sir Gridaud had turned his charger again and once more sped down on the Duke, and again the dust obscured the two figures for a second. When it had settled Sir Roger was still upon one knee but his great sword was bloody halfway up its four-foot blade and suddenly the Frenchman's horse collapsed beneath him and threw its rider to the ground. Blood welled from a huge slash in the charger's side and the animal tried hysterically to rise twice and then rolled on its side and lay still.

Sir Gridaud lay upon the ground a foot or two from his dead charger and there was a growl from the French faction, and a cheer from that of Grand Fenwick as Sir Roger approached his fallen adversary. But when he had come close to him, he stood his great sword in the ground by the point and walked to the fallen knight, helped him to his feet.

The Abbot groaned. "This old-fashioned courtesy of the, Duke's will be the death of him," he said. "He will die of good manners in an ill-bred world."

"'Twould not be a bad death at that," said Sir Dermot. "Since a man must die anyway, 'tis better to die for something he believes in than for nothing at all."

The Abbot looked at him sharply. "This from you?" he said.

"I begin to like the old knight," said Sir Dermot, "though he is an idiot to risk his neck, with all the responsibilities he has, over the hanging of a forester."

"There is more to it than that, as you will learn perhaps," said the Abbot. "Sir Roger fights here for his dukedom and his people."

They turned now to watch the two. Both were upon their feet again and had been brought each a cup of wine by the Herald of Chivalry. They pledged each other's health and drank the wine, though it was necessary for Sir Roger to remove his casque completely to drink his cup, since his visor was not hinged.

Then they turned once more to the combat, resumed now afoot.

Physically there was not much to choose between the two knights who now swung and hacked at each other with their fearful weapons. Sir Roger had an ox-like strength contained in a small solid body. Sir Gridaud was all sprung steel, taller than his opponent and quicker on his feet despite his massive plate armor. But at that there was not much footwork to their contest. They swung at each other, the one with the battle-ax and the other with the great sword, like two smiths beating upon anvils. The ring of the weapons came clearly across the lists, the note of the sword being higher and that of the battle-ax a deep and almost pleasant boom. But it soon became clear that Sir Gridaud had an advantage in his armor. Blow after blow of the great sword was turned by the steel plates of the Frenchman whereas Sir Roger dared not receive on his mail a blow of the ax, for it would have felled him in the moment.

His skill at parrying, however, was magnificent. Time and again he caught the bit of the ax on the blade of his sword and deflected the blow to the ground. His mighty shoulders heaved and rolled under their mail coat with the strain, but his short, thick legs were like the trunks of oak trees and it seemed that the contest must end only in one or the other of the knights becoming too exhausted to defend himself from the other's terrible weapon.

Sir Roger made himself the hub of a circle around which Sir Gridaud moved, flailing away, inch by inch. Blow after blow was delivered and avoided or parried and after two hours there was still no sign of either knight weakening. When the end came, it was with a suddenness that astonished the spectators.

Sir Gridaud, using his battle-ax in the manner of a scythe, swung blow after blow from side to side at Sir Roger, forcing him back to escape the arc of steel hurtling through the air before him. The onslaught was savage and in a measure desperate, and Sir Roger retreated for ten or fifteen paces, parrying as well as he could. Then he stopped, took the swing of the ax fully on his blade, stooped, and with a tremendous thrust, toppled Sir Gridaud over upon his back, the battle-ax wrenched from his grasp by the leverage of the big sword.

The Frenchman was given no time to rise. Sir Roger was over him immediately, a foot on each side of his chest. And then there was a cry of rage from Sir Gridaud's supporters and several of them, carrying cudgels, ducked under the barrier to come to the rescue of their lord.

They were quick, but not as quick as the Abbot. He was already in the list, his sleeves rolled up and his wicked mace brandished over his head.

"Back, scoundrels," he roared. "Back, you unshriven sinners. Hell's pit yearns for everyone of you. Lay hands on either knight and I'll make a pudding of your skulls."

He sensed someone beside him and half turned to see Sir Dermot leaning casually on his longbow with an arrow held ready for the string in his teeth. Whether it was the formidable presence of the

Abbot, or the equally formidable reputation with the longbow of the Irishman that caused the men to hesitate, is a moot point. But hesitate they did and then returned, grumbling, to the barrier.

Sir Roger now addressed the fallen Sir Gridaud and begged him to yield or be shriven and dispatched, since those were the terms under which they fought.

"At what will you set my ransom?" asked the Frenchman who, in common with his people, was practical as well as courageous.

"At one large cannon, six barrels of gunpowder and two of cannon shot," said Sir Roger.

"I yield," said Sir Gridaud. "You shall have the ransom."

Three days after the close of the tournament, when the brilliant international assemblage had returned to their own countries, and Sir Gridaud, having given his knight's oath to deliver his ransom within two weeks, had also been permitted to return to his home, two friars walked wearily up the Pass of Pinot from the French lands.

They were immediately seen from the watchtower and taken to Sir Roger.

"Well," said he, "what is your news?"

"Your Grace," they replied, "all you have heard of Formigny is true. The French are expert with this new weapon and have great numbers of it. And also they are coming against Grand Fenwick, in such a host as they have never massed before."

Sir Roger said nothing in reply. It was time now to call the representatives of his people together; time for him to tell them the whole truth; time to brace their flagging spirits for a critical struggle for their freedom in the face of a weapon of which they stood in dread.

He dismissed the friars and went slowly to the Virgin's Chapel and knelt before the altar. Sir Dermot passing and seeing him there thought even more highly of the stubborn, solid Englishman.

CHAPTER XII

THE Council of the Lords and Freemen of Grand Fenwick met in the Great Hall of the castle the day following the return of the two friars. Sir Roger, handsomely clad in a quilted doublet of blue, white great hose, and with a cotehardie of red velvet about his shoulders, itself trimmed with ermine, presided. On his right sat the Abbot Almin, representing the Lords Spiritual, and to his right, Sir Dermot, for he had been asked to attend to give further evidence, if need be, on the effectiveness of cannon. Sir Roger's opinion of the Irishman was now mixed. He knew him for an excellent bowman. He had had from the friars confirmation that Sir Dermot had indeed been at the field of Formigny. But he still suspected him of cowardice—both because he had attempted to sell his armor and because he had found excuse to stay out of the lists during the great tournament. Also the man wrote poetry and that, in Sir Roger's view, was an effeminate pastime.

To the left of the Duke were the Counts of Mountjoy and

Azule, together with the twin knights of Azule, now sufficiently recovered from their mid-air collision, which had heavily bruised them both, to attend. This completed the nobility of the council.

At right angles to the table at which Sir Roger and his nobles were seated, were two other tables, one at each end. Both were for the representatives of the Commons of Grand Fenwick. There were twenty of these—ten elected from among the winegrowers and ten elected from among the farmers, livestock raisers and tradespeople of the Duchy. They represented the two major agricultural interests of the Duchy and might be thought of as different though not necessarily opposing parties. David Bentner, a heavy man with dark hair streaked with white, was the leader of the livestock group and Francis Upworth, a smallish, very thin man in his silver-haired sixties, the leader of the winegrowers. These two parties were known commonly as the Pinots and the Lambs, though in fact they had no official title and no official existence, but were lumped together as the Commons.

Nicholas Breakspear, as secretary of the council, sat apart at a small table with an array of newly pointed goose-quill pens before him, and a large inkhorn resting upon a rack.

"My Lords and Commons," said Sir Roger when the buzz of greetings had died down, "is it your wish that the Great Sword be produced?"

"Aye," roared the Lords and Commons in unison.

The Great Sword, a much more elaborate weapon than Sir Roger had used at the tournament, once in place symbolized complete protection for any in the council chamber, who might then speak his mind overboldly, assured that there would be no revenge taken nor penalty enacted. The sword embodied in one weapon protection for the council members and assurance of the enforcement of their decisions.

The curtains at the end of the Great Hall parted and in came the sergeant at arms, carrying before him, like a cross, the Great Sword of Grand Fenwick. He was escorted by two men at arms with halberds. The Great Sword was placed on a table before Sir Roger and all stood until this was done and only when the sword had been laid upon the table did they resume their seats.

The sergeant and the two men at arms withdrew to the side of the hall, and Sir Roger, who had remained standing, looked around at the Commons at the two tables before him and cleared his throat with a loud "Harrumph." Sir Roger was no orator, and the Abbot had drilled him in a few phrases with which to lead up to the critical topic of discussion. But these phrases had escaped him now, and even had he recalled them, he would have thrown them aside as so much superfluous baggage. He had a soldier's mind, given to direct action and speech, and he waded right into his subject.

"My Lords and Commons," he said, "I have called you to this meeting to tell you officially what you perhaps already know, that the King of France has determined to try once more to conquer our land and is at this moment gathering an army for that purpose. We may expect his attack at the earliest in four weeks' time, for it will take him that long to muster his men and march across France to the Pass of Pinot. He will be bringing with him a great number of the same cannon which defeated the English army with heavy slaughter at the Field of Formigny, as you have heard from Sir Dermot of Ballycastle.

"He has vowed to annihilate this dukedom and to bring me in chains to Paris at the tail of a cart."

Having set forth the situation in plain terms, Sir Roger paused and from the Commons there came an uneasy shuffling of feet and men looked at the table before them rather than at their neighbors or Sir Roger. None wanted to say what all knew to be so—that no effective resistance could be offered by Grand Fenwick to the new French weapon and therefore that this was the end of the Duchy.

The reaction was so strange to his people that Sir Roger found difficulty in accepting it, though the Abbot had warned him what to expect, and he tried to rouse the assembly out of its gloom.

"Come, gentles," he said, "I have not known you downcast before at the prospect of having sport with the French. Bentner, what say you? You sit there as though you had just been measured for your coffin—and found the price too high." The sally would normally have brought a laugh, for Bentner was a man of great parsimony and it was an old joke in the Duchy that to pay for his coffin would be more grievous to him than the death that made the payment necessary.

"Your Grace," said Bentner. "I know nothing to say. We have all heard from Sir Dermot of the power of these cannon. His report is confirmed by the friars with whose news all here are acquainted. We are as defenseless as babes. There is nothing that can be done.

We have no weapon to use against the French."

"We have still the bow," said Sir Roger slowly. "It has served us handsomely in the past."

"Aye, Your Grace, but that was in the past. Now we cannot get within range of these cannon to loose our arrows. What man, Your Grace, do you think will advance through this hell's fire to do so? How many, so advancing, would survive? How many will even stand, knowing such a weapon is to be used against them? We of Grand Fenwick do not lack courage, but I believe that as soon as these cannon appear, you will find no army at your back."

"We are soon to have a cannon of our own in Grand Fenwick," said the Duke, playing his best card for he had kept this secret. He then announced what ransom he had set upon Sir Gridaud, Count of Chaux de Fonds. The announcement brought a flicker of interest, but no great revival of spirits.

"One cannon, Your Grace?" said Bentner. "Twenty might help—but one is nothing."

"It seems," said the Duke grimly, "that we in Grand Fenwick are already defeated by these French cannon though we have never seen one of them fired yet. The very word robs us of our manhood." He glared around at the Commons and found no echo of hardiness among them. Their depression and apathy filled him not with dismay but with wrath, and his face grew redder and he clenched his fists on the table before him.

"Hear me everyone of you," he roared, "It is fear and not weapons that strikes men down and I am warrior enough to know this. It is fear that enslaves men and costs them their liberty. Doubt before battle is more powerful than any cannon, and terror has destroyed more armies than all the weapons in the world.

"I do not seek to belittle these cannon of the French. Yet the French have a greater weapon than their cannon in your fears of it. Unless you can cast them out, you are lost before a shot is fired or an arrow fitted to a string. And," he thundered, "you deserve to be lost. For the world is not a place for timid men, nor is liberty a birthright of those who fear to fight and speak for it come what may. Nor was this dukedom founded by men who hung back from the assault. If we lose Grand Fenwick now, let us admit that we lost it through fear and not through gunshot and let us admit that we deserve to lose it, for it is no place to be held by cowards. And let us admit that we were not men enough to hand this land of ours on to our sons."

There was a grumbling murmur from among the Commons, for they had no liking to be called cowards by their Duke.

Robin Goodspeed got up and said, angrily, "Your Grace knows I would follow you into Hell and so will many of my fellows."

"Aye," said the Duke. "I know it indeed. But thinking you were following me into Hell, you would come somewhat cautiously. I want hard, lusty fighting men at my back baring their teeth at death, when the French come. I want no nervous men, secretly praying for surrender and terms of mercy. I want men who have to be held in on the leash; not men who have to be tugged forward by it."

Francis Upworth, leader of the winegrowers, cleared his throat nervously and asked leave to speak.

"Your Grace," he said, "you say the French king comes against us and with a mighty host. Cannon or no cannon, we must either resist or surrender. Is there no other way? Is it not possible to treat with the King of France, to see what he desires of us and see what terms of his we can meet and still survive?"

The Abbot replied to the question for Sir Roger.

"The French terms, I have learned from our two friars, are that this dukedom be annexed to the King of France, that all here swear loyalty to the French king, and that Sir Roger be surrendered to his mercy, and that a duke of the French king's choosing be put over us. Is it your wish to accept these terms?"

There was a shout of "No" from the assembly, and for the first time during the meeting, Sir Roger smiled.

"Well then," continued Upworth, "can we not obtain allies to help us resist the French? The Dauphin controls his own lands and runs his own kingdom on our borders. He is a rebel against his father. Could we not ask his aid? I am sure that he must have some of these cannon also, since the Count of Chaux de Fonds, whose estates lie in Dauphiné, has provided us with one for his ransom."

"Then would our freedom depend upon the Dauphin," said Sir Roger, "and that would be no freedom at all but dependence, for the son is as avaricious as the father. What allies would we have against our allies? No. That is the wrong road. We have always in the past fought our wars alone and so have retained our independence. An alliance with the Dauphin would be the first step toward becoming subjects of the Dauphin, and there would be an end to Grand

Fenwick."

The old Count of Azule turned to Sir Dermot. If he still harbored any resentment over the humiliation of his two sons he did not show it now, and neither did they.

"Sir Knight," he said, "what counsel have you for us? You alone of all those present have seen these cannon used in battle. Is there any means wherewith they can be withstood?"

"I can tell you only how they may *not* be withstood," said Sir Dermot. "And that is by using the old methods of fighting which have been the fashion for the past hundred years. But I fancy that, with thought, some method of prevailing against them may be devised. You are not here, in Grand Fenwick, without some advantages which we lacked at Formigny, for there we met the French on the open field. Here are mountains for walls and your Pass of Pinot is no easy road for these cannon. Something might be hit upon by wise heads. But as Sir Roger has stated, it will not be work for timid men. Your archers must be prepared to face these cannon, if they are to prevail against them. And they are no easy weapon to face. They will unnerve the staunchest."

"Would they unnerve you?" Sir Roger shot at him.

"To stand against them as we did at Formigny—yes," said the Irishman. "I tell you plainly that I would not do it. For that is sure death."

Sir Roger snorted.

"Though every man in my dukedom turned craven," he said, "I would stand against them and openly."

"If you put your head in a bear's mouth, you do not prove yourself either wise or brave but only foolish," said Sir Dermot hotly. It looked for a second as if a quarrel would develop between the two, there and then, and perhaps to avert it, Piers of the Glebe got up in his deliberate plowman's way, and leaned his two fists on the table before him and rubbed his ill-shaven jowl on his hunched-forward shoulder, which was ever a sign with Piers that he had a thought to offer.

"Your Grace," he said, "we have with us the Abbot Almin and I believe he has some part to play here. For it seems to me that this new method of killing, whereby someone a great distance off can destroy his fellows on the moment and they defenseless, may well run contrary to the will of God. For here is a very devilish kind of slaughter, and a very unnatural one."

Piers paused and ran a thick tongue over his lips, as if by wetting them to ease out the words which formed only slowly in his mind out of the vague substance of his thoughts.

"Now, my lord," he said, "dealing with the parts of which this gunpowder is made—we all do know that this same niter, as the Abbot hath told us, put to a more proper purpose greatly enriches the land. For I do use it myself for raising peas and marrows and other goodly vegetables. It hath then a dual purpose or use—one good and the other evil, as I believe have all things given by God to man for his use.

"Now this being so, and it being granted that it must be evil in the sight of God to blow up our fellows with that which is best used to raise cabbages, could not His Grace the Abbot, consulting with others of the Church, produce a ban upon the use of this weapon by all Christian nations in the name of God Whom we must all serve? This ban, coming from Mother Church, would surely end warfare by this means."

The Abbot shook his head and it was plain that he was angry.

"Were all Christians Christian," he snorted, "such a ban would be unnecessary. Since they are not, it would be ineffective. And do not let us prick ourselves on our piety here, and think we are more noble than the French. For we would certainly use these cannon had we in Grand Fenwick as many incrusted stable walls as there are in France. We would invoke God's ban because we are short of niter, and here is a kind of a foul blasphemy."

These considerations Sir Roger thought beside the point. The point as he saw it was a plain one and he proposed to get an answer to it without delay. Details could be considered later.

"Well, my Lords and Commons," he said, "what say you? Do we resist and with good heart, knowing our case is just? Or do we send emissaries to the French king begging his clemency and surrendering the dukedom? Let those who would resist cry 'Aye.'"

The response was thunderous. Hardly a man in the Great Hall but felt that in supporting the Duke he was signing his death warrant. And yet support him they did, for they loved him and the dukedom over which he reigned and which was their homeland.

"Here is better cheer," said Sir Roger, smiling. "Half the force of France was scattered with that vote. We have but to deal with a tawdry few—perhaps thirty thousand and a score of cannon. With your leave, gentles, I will send to the French defiance and a warning to keep their army away from the Pass of Pinot lest they receive a mangling they cannot afford."

"Your Grace," said Robin Goodspeed, "send no written messages, for few here can write. Send to the French captain what we can understand, and he also."

He reached down to the floor.

"Send him this, Your Grace," he said. And he held aloft a cloth-yard arrow, new-fletched with the feathers of the wild goose.

CHAPTER XIII

SIR DERMOT of Ballycastle, in the days immediately following the crucial meeting of the Council of Freemen, was left much to his own devices. Sir Roger, in frequent consultation with the Abbot, the Count of Azule and the Count of Mountjoy, and some of the leaders of the Commons, never asked for the advice of the foreign knight. His reasons were mixed. He did not like the Irishman, for one thing. Then, Sir Dermot was a foreigner and so might not properly be consulted about the defense of the Duchy. Again, Sir Dermot had made no attempt to conceal the fact that his sword had always in the past been for hire and Sir Roger wanted no mercenaries in his army. Finally, Sir Roger believed the Irishman afraid of the cannon. For his part Sir Dermot gave no sign of being offended by being thus cold-shouldered and enjoyed himself hugely.

He went hunting or hawking or fishing each day, sometimes with the Abbot when not otherwise engaged, but more often with the Lady Matilda and the Lady Janice. As a protection against matrimony, however, Sir Dermot never went alone with the Lady Matilda and, as a further protection, he often enlisted the services of the young groom in the castle as a page, and this young man had instructions to accompany the Irishman on most of his rides.

Despite these precautions, however, the Irishman had had some bad moments. The Lady Matilda had become something of an expert at getting into predicaments from which she had to be rescued. She was a constant victim of a runaway horse, and contrived to be thrown so many times that she was black and blue. And when Sir Dermot, in knightly courtesy, overtook her horse, or helped her back in the saddle, he found her looks so fond and her lips so moist and her eyes so tender and her face so fair that he had to conjure up for himself very quickly the remembrance of his married friend Sir Kevin of Rathgorm with his seventeen unwed daughters, to escape the peril of the altar that loomed before him.

As for the Lady Matilda, she became downright vexed at being rescued so frequently with nothing gained from it but a few bruises, and decided that she must try something more desperate, and preferably unconnected with horses. She thought of the Abbot and the lake and decided that here might be profitable material.

She was, however, making more progress with Sir Dermot than she guessed or he was prepared to admit.

At times in his apartments the Irish knight found himself thinking of the Lady Matilda, of the special grace of her figure, and the smooth line of her forearm, which was a miracle of elegance, and an especial way she had of raising one eyebrow very slightly when mildly surprised. And once or twice he had framed a few lines of verse about her, verse full of Irish extravagances such as:

> A leaf of oak hath fallen on
> My lady's breast.
> And all the oaks since dawn of time
> Were in this blest.
> For every oak that ever grew
> Since world began
> Served to produce this single leaf,
> More blest than man.

This verse and others like it he set to music, and since he was no man to hide such talents, he sang his verses, accompanying himself upon the lute, to the Lady Matilda (and the Lady Janice) and found himself in greater peril than ever.

Each day he resolved that on the following day he would bid goodbye to Sir Roger and leave for Florence, perhaps taking Nicholas Breakspear with him for company on the road. But each day he postponed his departure with arguments which were beginning to sound uncomfortably convincing.

"Ah, Dermot, me boy," he would say, "don't go making the mistake ye've been making all yer life—running away from food and shelter because ye're frightened by a girl that's heartsick."

Or he would say, looking at himself in a steel mirror, "Dermot, do ye think that the whole of life is nothing but a trip from fight to fight and table to table and hill to hill with a few intervals sleeping under hedges and such? Isn't it time ye settled down and were a credit to yer people as a sober, God-fearing man with never a cross word from ye from sunrise to sunset? Answer me now. What'll ye be doing when ye're sixty if ye're still on the road when ye're forty?"

And sometimes he would say, "'Twould be nice to have a place of me own that has been landless all me life—somewhere I could shut the door against the wind and tell me children what a great warrior I was when I was their age."

Having given himself some such argument as this, and been shaken by the force of it, Sir Dermot would glare fiercely at himself in the mirror, vow that regular food and a warm bed were making him soft, and vow also that he would be on the road to Florence by the morrow at the latest.

But the days went by and he did not take the road to Florence.

One day Sir Dermot, the Abbot Almin and the Lady Matilda went fishing together in the Lady Deep. Sir Dermot agreed to the fishing venture since the Abbot would be present, and he believed that the Abbot would protect him with the protection he needed from the Lady Matilda. They had taken out a flat-bottomed boat which was anchored in the center of the lake and were fishing for a pike which the Abbot swore lived in a hole in the bottom of the lake over which the boat was anchored.

"His name," the Abbot said, "is Bentnose, and my predecessor fished for him twenty years and hooked him but once. I have fished for him these twenty-five years and hooked him twice and once had him all but gaffed when he struck against the side of the boat, shook the hook from his mouth and was gone.

"He's the greatest pike in the whole of Europe. 'Tis said that the crown of King Leofranc is in his belly, it having been thrown into the lake when the king was escaping from his enemies. He is a yard and a half long if he is an inch, and as fierce as a boar in the springtime…"

"He's not the biggest pike in all Europe at all," said Sir Dermot fondling one end of his huge mustache and giving a little wink at the Lady Matilda seated between them. "The biggest pike in all Europe was in Lough Erne in Ireland and 'twas meself that caught it when ten years of age. I'd been fishing," he added, "five minutes."

"Humph," said the Abbot. "A minnow no doubt or some miserable salmon's sprat for which you should have been flogged without mercy for taking it from the water."

"No minnow. No salmon's sprat," said the Irishman. "The biggest pike in all Europe. And do ye know how I come to say that?"

"I do not," said Almin.

"Because," said the Irishman, "'twas no miserable king's crown that it had in its belly but a bishop's miter and the bishop as well," and he let out a great roar of laughter, shaking the boat and bringing pleas from the Abbot to be quiet or he would certainly frighten Bentnose away.

"This pike," said the Abbot, "hath habits of the most cunning kind and I believe his intelligence is not much below that of a human being. He has been fished so long that he is cautious of every morsel of food that comes his way. And when he catches a fish or a young duckling he will run with the tidbit held in his lips for several hundred yards until he is certain there is no hook in it. Then he will take it lightly in his mouth and lie quiet awhile, tasting it and still in some doubt. And it is only when he is sure that there is no hook that he will swallow his food. These habits, slowing down his feeding, make him hungry at all times, but especially on such a day as this when the water is bright under the sun and the fish, which are his normal prey, do not venture to swim about in it, but lie, each of them in his own nest.

"Therefore," continued the Abbot, "when you see your float sink, loose the line and keep it loosed for the space of two Pater Nosters said slowly. To these add three Ave Marias at a medium pace, and if your line is still taken gently through the water at the end of that time, strike like a Moor to bed your hook deep in his gullet and then give him play, and I will pray for you. Or perhaps I had better bring him in."

"Pshaw," said Sir Dermot, "'tis plain you'll never catch this pike for that is not the way to go about it at all. Let him have but a nibble, but enough to make your float twinkle on the water, and then strike with a scream like an eagle, and he is yours, every gleaming, scaly foot of him."

"Yes, Sir Dermot," said the Lady Matilda to the Abbot's annoyance, for she had always taken her fishing instructions from him. She gave the knight a look which was a caress and he turned to watch his float and silence settled over the three of them and the waters of the Lady Deep.

The sun was warm, the boat rocked gently making minute music along its sides. The mountains around, blue green and silver, seemed because of this rocking to undulate gently, and soon the Abbot had fallen asleep. Sir Dermot decided that safety for him lay in pretending to follow suit. He put his long legs over one gunwale of the boat, braced his back against the other, let his chin fall on his chest, closed his eyes and in a few minutes his pretense had become a reality and he had dosed off, snoring slightly.

He was awakened by a violent shaking of the boat and a loud scream and opened his eyes to see the Lady Matilda teetering, clawing for her balance, at the side of the boat. He caught but a glimpse of her and, sprawled as he was, was unable to help. In a second she had gone over the side.

Sir Dermot struggled to his feet in the rocking boat, embracing the Abbot for support.

"Give him play!" roared the Abbot.

"That pike is well hooked, I believe," cried the Irishman, and over he went, all arms and legs, after the Lady Matilda. There was a current flowing through the Lady Deep caused by the river which fed it at one end and which tended to empty it at the other. When Sir Dermot came up he was ten or fifteen feet from the boat and looked like an ill-fed walrus with his long mustaches drooped down below his chin. He caught a glimpse of the Lady Matilda's head—just the golden crown of it—twenty feet away and splashed and churned toward her.

"Hold onto him," he roared. "Hold on now. I'm coming up to you like a salmon," and, dragged down by his clothing, he struggled and floundered half above and half below the water until he reached the spot. But the Lady Matilda had disappeared and he put his head down in the water and glimpsed her below him. Down the Irishman went, seized her around the shoulders and lifted her up.

"Where's the rod?" he cried. "You didn't let go of it now, did you?"

The Lady Matilda's face was toward him as he spoke and he looked at her, pale and lovely and streaming with water. Her fair hair, now darkened to the color of honey, framed her features and her slim white neck, and quite suddenly he saw her as if for the first time and forgot about the fish.

"Holy Mother of God," he said reverently, "you're beautiful."

He bent the Lady Matilda's head toward him and kissed her, first on the cheek and then on the mouth, and he felt in that kiss that they would never be two people again, and that each breath he drew strengthened her as it did him. In his arms she felt as slim as a peeled willow wand and as light as a child and for the first time in his life he felt a deep serenity and happiness which filled every empty, lonely fiber in him.

The Abbot brought over the boat and scolded the Lady Matilda for losing the pike and for falling overboard and got her tenderly into the boat and glowered at Sir Dermot. But neither she nor Sir Dermot said anything to each other all the time that it took to reach the castle.

The Lady Matilda went to her apartments, to change her clothing, like one in a dream, and Sir Dermot went to the stables.

"Saddle the Mare of Cashel," he told the groom. "I'm going to Florence."

"All wet like that?" asked the groom.

"Yes," said the Irishman. "If I stay another moment I'm a lost man."

CHAPTER XIV

SIR DERMOT of Ballycastle had his back to a cliff, his battered shield before him on his left arm, and with his right arm was swinging and cutting and parrying and thrusting with his great sword at four or five rascals armed with ironbound cudgels and one of them with a piece of chain, who had beset him.

While he fought he roared—insults, shouts for succor, snatches of prayers and occasionally a bit of song when some particular stroke of his came off roundly.

His efforts went in some such manner as this:

"A limb of the ugliest limb of Satan, ye are. God turned his back on the world the day ye were spawned in some cesspit. A chain is it? Ooouch. Holy Mary, Mother of God, was I so bad that ye desert me now? I hadn't the money for a candle and that is why I didn't light one to thee the last time. Take that"—with a swipe of the sword—"and look around for yer hand. It has yer cudgel in it. Three of ye together is it? Ah…it's sinful I've been all the days of me life and here's the reckoning. Isn't there an angel in heaven not too busy to spare a thought for an Irishman with his back to a heathen mountain and five devils at his throat? Arooo! Me arm won't take another stroke like that! 'Tis all fire now and every muscle sobbing with agony. A succor! A succor! Dermot abu! A Dermot! A Dermot!

"Ah now. That was prettily done. Four fingers at one stroke is not to be sneezed at. Devil take the man with the chain. There's more dents in me helmet than in a tavern tankard. Mother Mary, I'm on me knees and getting weaker. Send two of the Apostles and pick strong ones for I need them now. A succor! A succor!"

The Irishman had indeed been beaten to his knees. He had disposed of two of his attackers but the other three flayed at him, one with a chain and two with cudgels, and it was all he could do to ward off some of the blows with his battered shield. And at the moment when he felt he must surely go to whatever reward the Lord had in store for such a man as he, it seemed that his prayers were answered.

From behind the three brigands appeared a figure garbed in a cowl and black robe who let out a great shout and charged into the fray.

"Ah Holy Mother," said the Irishman, "I thank you. One of the stout sons of Zebedee. I always had a fancy for them."

But it was not one of the sons of Zebedee who had come to his aid but the Abbot Almin, who, calling upon the Almighty with some confidence to guard the right, laid about him so busily with his cudgel that the three knaves sped, leaving one of their fellows dead on the field and the other limping off behind them.

"You are well come," said the Irishman, taking off his battered casque which he threw upon the ground and immediately seated himself beside it. "Five minutes more and I would have been passing the time of day with St. Peter and politely inquiring after me mother and father."

"'Tis no wish of mine that I'm here," said the Abbot, seating himself beside the knight.

"The Pope hath sent for you for instructions on the habits of trout?" asked the Irishman. "'Twill go ill with you in Rome if it is known how much time you spend in the Lady Deep and how little in the Lady Chapel. But I'll befriend ye. Accept demotion to a brother and ye can pass around the plate when I'm playing me lute and we'll divide the spoils and share and share alike."

"Bah," snorted the Abbot. "Oh that I should use my declining strength to save such a rogue. Had I arrived but two minutes later I could have returned and reported you dead."

"Ye could have stood aside two minutes and produced the same effect," said the Irishman.

"I could have," said the Abbot moodily, "but I am a weak and greedy man and easily overcome by temptation. I have never been able to stand aside and see one man get all the fight while another got none."

"I'm thinking ye might get to Heaven, for there is likely Irish blood in yer veins," said Sir Dermot.

"God and all his holy angels forbid it," said the Abbot. "I come of decent churchgoing, law-abiding, bloodthirsty English stock.

There's no whining Celt in me."

"If I were not so tired," said Sir Dermot, "and if you were not a churchman, I would split your head open."

"You may forget about me being a churchman," said the Abbot.

"Ah well," said Sir Dermot, "I'm still tired. And I think you a friend for you saved me life."

"I will regret it all my days," said the Abbot.

"We talk in circles," said the Irishman. "What brings you here?"

"You," replied the Abbot.

"Me?"

"Yes. You. I am to take you back to Grand Fenwick."

"And just for the sake of argument supposing that I don't wish to go to Grand Fenwick, me path lying toward Florence?"

"Just for the sake of argument," said the Abbot fiercely, "I'd knock you over the head and take you there anyway."

"Would you now?" said Sir Dermot. "You tempt me, man. Let me get me wind a little and perhaps ye can try that trick. And while I'm getting me wind perhaps ye'll be so good as to explain the reason for this great desire to have me return to Grand Fenwick. Is it perhaps to fight Sir William of Azule and Sir Derek and provide a little sport for the Duchy?"

"No," said the Abbot. "It is not. It is because the Lady Matilda (may the Holy Mother of God protect her from all harm) is weeping out her eyes because you have gone away and will not be persuaded, even by her old friend and confessor, that your departure was but

God's way of removing her from harm."

"I will not go back to the Lady Matilda," said Sir Dermot. He said it softly but with fervor. "I will not go back for if I do I am a lost man and the open road is taken from me and the sweetness of the bracken and the sight of great plains with lakes upon them like garments of silver, and the beckoning of the mountains. I will not go back."

"I wish I had found you dead," said the Abbot.

"I wish so too," said the Irishman.

The Abbot looked at him curiously. "Why so?" he asked.

"Because," said the Irishman, "though you are too old and stiff and crabbed and English to understand it, I walk about now as a dead man—only worse than dead. What is alive of me is separated from my body and in another place and it has cried out to me every yard of this weary road to come back. Every step of my horse has said, 'Don't go on. Don't go on,' and every echo that has come back has said, 'Turn back. Turn back.' And yet I have dragged myself along like a corpse looking for its grave so that I can pull the earth over my ears and not hear these pleadings any more."

"You love her?" asked the Abbot in amazement.

"Do you suppose I would leave her else?" demanded the knight fiercely.

"Do you suppose that such a man as I, the owner of one battered suit of armor and not as much land as could be covered by the hoofs of the Mare of Cashel would leave a lady such as she—an angel sweeter than all the springtimes upon God's earth—unless he loved her? Why, man, did I not love her I would be in Grand Fenwick now, plucking on me lute and composing odes and playing courtier and robbing as delicately and heavily as I might…of her purse and other treasures which she has.

"Before God I love her and always will. And therein is me blessing and me curse. So let me on the road to Florence and do you return to the Lady Matilda and tell her you found me dead. But if you fear the fires of Hell do not say that I loved her."

"This puts another cast upon the whole matter," said the Abbot. "I took you for but a witty rogue who had his pleasure of Grand Fenwick and was now on his way to see what tales he could spin of Grand Fenwick in Florence."

"I'll say nothing of Grand Fenwick in Florence. But if there I can find some service with the Medici of a dangerous sort then will I offer them my sword."

"I thought you set upon playing the lute?"

"'Twas but a passing fancy," said the Irishman. "I like the music of steel better. It gives aches to the body but relieves those of the heart."

"And yet you must return to Grand Fenwick," said the Abbot. "Now more than ever."

"I am for Florence, I say," said the Irishman.

"Then we must fight," said the Abbot.

"I've had a belly of fighting for one day," said Sir Dermot.

"You turn craven?"

"In this matter, yes."

"It is common report in Grand Fenwick that your liver is white," said the Abbot. "I now suspect different, but Sir Roger holds you fled the field of Formigny and the people say you fled Grand Fenwick because the French are coming with their cannon."

"A man knows what he is—coward or brave," said Sir Dermot. "What others say of him is either true or false and does not alter the case."

"Yet Sir Roger would not give you the hand of the Lady Matilda if he thought you coward."

"Then let him think me coward," said Sir Dermot, "for I flee the hand of the Lady Matilda."

"Because of the road you talk of and the plains and the mountains?"

"I tell meself that is why," said the Irishman.

"But these are torture to you now."

"They are, at that."

"There comes a time when they are torture to all men and they must turn their backs to them and seek their love, and so the will of God is served and families begotten under the sanction of Holy Matrimony."

"Seventeen and all of them girls," groaned Sir Dermot.

The significance of this remark escaped the Abbot. He eyed the Irishman who had risen stiffly and with a groan and was walking toward his horse. The Abbot muttered a prayer for guidance so that he might best serve the interests of his beloved Lady Matilda and said, "I've heard that all the Irish live with pigs, except their knights who are permitted the use of English cowsheds."

He heard Sir Dermot draw in his breath sharply, but the knight still thrust his foot into the stirrup.

"It is common knowledge," continued the Abbot, "that the part of an Irishman in battle is to pillage and rob those who have fallen to the swords of the English."

"God give me strength," muttered Sir Dermot fiercely, seating himself in the saddle.

"The women of the Irish," shouted the Abbot, "are known to be anxious to warm the bed of any Scottish tinker who comes down the road."

"DRAW!" roared Sir Dermot. "Draw! For by Our Lady, I will bury you this night."

"Thanks be to God," said the Abbot. He rolled up the flowing sleeves of his robe, revealing thick strong arms, hitched his skirts up firmly under his belt to give better play to his feet and stood, his legs apart and his cudgel held firmly before him.

Sir Dermot, knowing the Abbot was unarmored, discarded his cuirass, gauntlets and greaves and seized a cudgel of the man who had fallen.

"Pray!" roared the Irishman and came at him.

"Lord," whispered the Abbot, "do not let me crack him too hard upon his wineskin."

The fight lasted only five minutes. Sir Dermot was more tired and hurt from his previous encounter than he knew and slipped to one knee.

"*Requiescat in pace—pro tempore*," said the Abbot and tapped him on the skull, and the Irishman slumped quite gently to the ground.

The Abbot stood for a moment over him, looking down to make sure that there was no fight left in Sir Dermot.

"My son," he said, "you are called, even as I was, to repentance and decent Christian living—though in your case I do not think that the call came too early."

CHAPTER XV

SIR DERMOT arrived back in Grand Fenwick supported in a litter which the Abbot had contrived for him. He was too severely bruised to ride his horse and he developed a fever so that the churchman was worried and at times stormed at him to play the man and get well and at other times beseeched him not to die.

"If you die," said the Abbot, when he had put the Irishman in the litter and strapped the poles to the two horses, "I fear the Lady Matilda will die also."

But Sir Dermot, at the time, had not quite recovered his senses, between the knocks on the head he had taken and the fever which was on him. He only replied, "Seventeen girls…impossible to keep them virgins…"

This aggravated the Abbot, who puzzled a great deal about it; the more so since Sir Dermot kept talking about these mysterious seventeen girls and at every mention groaned deeply as if sorely afflicted in his spirits.

"I must get a full confession from him, for there is some sin upon his soul which troubles him," the Abbot said. So he determined to attend to the nursing of Sir Dermot himself. Being skilled in letting blood and applying plasters so hot that, as he put it, the departing soul experiencing a foretaste of Hell decided not to quit the body at that time, he had Sir Dermot upon his feet though somewhat shaky in less than a week.

One morning, when his patient had recovered sufficiently to roar that if another plaster was laid upon him he would drive the Abbot's head through the wall, the good man questioned the Irishman about the seventeen girls.

"It is not mete," he said, "on the eve of your nuptials to dwell upon the conquests of the past. Besides, seventeen for a man of your age is a poor score, particularly since you have traveled much, stopping but a night or two in any one place. Before a premature repentance overcame me, I had easily exceeded that number—may God forgive me."

"You have taken leave of your wits," said the Irishman. "What are you talking about…seventeen girls?"

The Abbot explained that all through his late illness Sir Dermot had kept repeating "seventeen girls," to which he had added that it was impossible to keep them virgins.

"Now," he continued, "I am not to be taken as supporting the seduction of virgins, though it is a certainty that unless they are betrothed at eight or nine and kept close eye upon thereafter until their marriage, they will certainly be seduced. Yet if it has been your lot to seduce seventeen virgins you are entitled to this consolation—that you did but take upon yourself seventeen sins against chastity which must otherwise have been committed by others, and thus have saved seventeen of your fellow men from putting their souls in mortal peril. Mysterious are the ways of the Lord. It is easier to bring one man to repentance than seventeen—to save one soul than to save seventeen souls. And I see in this the workings of Divine Grace, for you are, I am sure, close to repentance of your transgressions. Therefore are seventeen sins forgiven in one man to the glory of God and the strengthening of his Church.

"Come, my son, make a full confession now upon your knees and receive the absolution of your confessor."

"Sir Abbot," said the knight, "I have often warned you against the practice of keeping your bait in your mouth so that they might be the livelier for your fishing. Now it seems that the worms have eaten into your brains as I had feared and you have become half-mad."

"Mad!" said the Abbot impatiently. "It is you who have been mad this past week with your prattling about these seventeen virgins."

Sir Dermot sighed and his eyes, which had contained up to then a sparkle of life and interest, became dull.

"Aha," said the Abbot, noting this, "the sin withheld burns ten times more fiercely than when confessed freely to the unworthy servant of a merciful God to whom has been given the gift of remission of sins, both venial and mortal."

"It is not me," said Sir Dermot, "but me friend Sir Kevin of

Rathgorm, whose own fate has clearly foreshadowed the doom which lies ahead of me."

"If one knight seduce seventeen, it is not required of his brother in arms to match the figure," said the Abbot.

"If you would keep your preaching out of your conversation we would get along better," said Sir Dermot, and told the doleful story of Sir Kevin of Rathgorm and his seventeen unwed daughters.

"Why here is foolishness to cap all of Twelfth Night," said the Abbot. "Do you suppose that because Sir Kevin hath been cursed for his sins with seventeen daughters the same fate will overtake you?"

"I have been an equal sinner," said Sir Dermot.

"Pshaw," said the Abbot. "Put it out of your mind. The Lord hath more imagination than to repeat his punishments. Some other penance will be meted out to you in due course. Mayhap you will have seventeen sons who will be broiling and fighting and roaring about in your old age so that you have not a moment's peace. Also you will have to supply them with seventeen horses and seventeen suits of armor and will be put to heavy expense. But should you have seventeen daughters and be living here in Grand Fenwick, then it would be simple to establish a nunnery and stock it with your own brood. We have need of a nunnery, for the friars are taken from their prayers by the need to wash their shirts."

Sir Dermot brightened. "Do you think I might have seventeen sons?" he asked.

"You have an equal chance of sons as daughters," said the Abbot. "If I judge you rightly you have never quailed before equal odds. Why does your heart fail you now?"

"Seventeen sons," said Sir Dermot, sitting up quite briskly in bed. "How strange that I had thought all this time of daughters. Why with seventeen sons to teach to ride and to wrestle and use the broadsword and spear the wild boar and cast the eagle—for it's eagles we hunt with in Ireland and not your tame falcons and goshawks and peregrines—I would be in seventeen heavens. One I would call Briari after the noble king that drove the Danes out of Ireland; and another Finn after the greatest warrior that ever lived; and a third Oisin after he who went to the Land of the Ever Young; and another…"

He was still naming his sons when the Abbot left him and was struggling between Cormac and Rory for the seventeenth when the Lady Matilda entered.

She looked so downcast and woeful that the Irishman stopped his speculations immediately and asked what was the trouble.

"Ah and lackaday," said the Lady Matilda, "the Duke, my father, has forbidden the match except on such terms that you cannot meet them."

"What are his terms?" demanded Sir Dermot. "I'll meet them in the hour and then have some breakfast, for I'm tired of soup and plasters."

"Ah, my love," said her ladyship. "He thinks you coward and so has set a task that would quail the heart of the sternest knight in the world."

"If he wants me to fight Sir William and Sir Derek," said Sir

Dermot, "prepare graves for them."

"It is more than that," said the Lady Matilda.

"More than that?"

"Even more."

The knight scratched his head. "He wants me to fight him?" he said.

"No. It is even more than that."

"He wants me to fight him and the Abbot?"

"No. Even more."

"There can't be more than that," said the Irishman.

"Alas," said Lady Matilda, "you little know my sire. He has persuaded himself that you ran from the Battle of Formigny at the first appearance of these cannon and therefore was saved and lived to tell the tale. He is persuaded also that you fled Grand Fenwick, fearing the coming of the French. Therefore, he calls you both coward and deserter of your fellows in arms and says that until you remove this taint and blot upon your shield he will never consent to giving you my hand."

"Well, does he want me to fight the Battle of Formigny all over again?" asked Sir Dermot.

"Something of that sort," said the Lady Matilda.

"I am beginning to feel ill again at the thought of it," said the knight. "But tell me how he expects me to achieve this?"

"Ah, my love," said Lady Matilda, "the Duke has ruled that my hand is to be given to you in marriage on condition that you stand before the great cannon, which is even now on its way here, while it

159

is discharged and defy it in the name of Grand Fenwick and the older order of knighthood."

"My lord Abbot," said the Irishman, "was here but a minute before and blithe as a lark. He made no mention of this condition but spoke of our coming nuptials."

"I have spoken to him upon the matter," said the Lady Matilda, "and he has said he is confident that you will accept the challenge. Yet I beg of you, dear Sir Dermot, to refuse it. Rather let us both flee in the night together and I will be your love until God takes us both to Heaven."

"I'll not be walking the roads of the world with seventeen sons trudging behind me demanding horses," said Sir Dermot. "And I begin to be angered at your gracious sire, the Duke, that he should doubt the courage of an Irishman, which is superior to the courage of any man on earth. So I will go to the Duke and accept his challenge."

"Ah, no," wailed the Lady Matilda. "No. You will be killed."

"Devil a bit of it," said Sir Dermot. "I was born to be hung and have no real fear of cannon—though the noise makes me nervous."

He hustled the Lady Matilda out of the room, clad himself and hurried off to find the Duke, a little wobbly on his legs, but whistling a little jig.

"Your Grace," he said, "I have come from me sickbed to ask the hand of your daughter, the Lady Matilda, in marriage. And in return I do give me life unto her service and pledge her me sword for her guarding, and will keep her safe from all her enemies and fight side by side with you against the French."

The Duke smiled in anticipation of the change he expected to see in this popinjay within the minute.

"You have not, Sir Knight," he said, "heard the conditions which I have laid down and which must be fulfilled before I will give my daughter in marriage."

"Some bit of a thing about standing in front of a cannon? Yes. I've heard of them."

"And you accept?" asked the Duke, astonished.

"I do," said Sir Dermot.

The Abbot was present, smiling the while, though succeeding at the same time in looking enormously innocent and impartial.

"Hath this man recovered from his illness?" Sir Roger asked. "Or have his wits left him?"

"He is recovered, Your Grace," said the Abbot.

"And he is not drunk?"

"Only with love for the Lady Matilda," said the knight.

"You have no counterconditions to ask?" the Duke inquired.

"One," said the Irishman.

"And what is that?"

"That you stand beside me before the cannon, for you would not have it said, Your Grace, that there is in your dukedom a man braver than yourself."

"Oh, you wily knave," roared the Duke. "I knew there was some trick here to send you hopping to me as gay as a jackdaw. But know you this, Sir Knight, that my courage has never been in question and is not in question now, for it is well known there is no bolder man in Grand Fenwick than myself."

"I fancy ye look at a bolder one now," said Sir Dermot. "Your Grace has taken leave to question me courage and I take the same leave to question yours."

"Holy Mother of God," roared the Duke. "Do you challenge me?"

"To stand beside me before the cannon—yes," said Sir Dermot, "though if you do not care to look at it I will stand in front and you may keep place behind me."

"Out of here, you rascal—OUT!" roared Sir Roger.

"Not, Your Grace, until I have your answer—or until you withdraw your opposition to me suit."

Sir Roger's face, as remarked previously, was naturally red. But now it glowed a deeper color which went down his neck and spread slowly to the tips of his ears. And then his color changed from a deeper red to purple, and he rose from his seat, sat again, rose once more, sat once more, and all the while clenched and unclenched his fists on the table before him.

The very sight of this performance would have reduced many a man in the dukedom to nervous collapse. But the Irishman looked steadily at the Duke out of his blue eyes and then pulled the end of one of his long mustaches as if studying the performance and deeply interested in it.

"What say you, Your Grace?" asked Sir Dermot at last.

"I say," said the Duke, each word struggling through the thickness of his anger, "that no man has lived to call me coward or challenge my courage..."

"The same with me," said Sir Dermot.

"...and I say that I will stand before this cannon with you and should we meet in Hell one moment after, I will beat you to the ground, you impudent puppy, amid the glowing coals."

"Ah now," said the Irishman, "don't take such a gloomy view of it. Ye might go to Heaven and be able to set after me with a harp."

CHAPTER XVI

WHEN the cannon arrived it was the wonder of Grand Fenwick. It was a huge piece weighing four tons and had to be hauled up the Pass of Pinot from France on a massive sled drawn by sixteen pair of draft horses. This sled was in fact its mounting. No axle nor pair of wheels could at that time be devised to support such a weight. The cannon was supported by huge lugs or trunnions on a framework of solid oak on the sled. It could be elevated by putting a number of wedges under the barrel and driving these home with a mallet, and there was on one side a pointer and a section of a circle to indicate the amount of elevation thus achieved.

But there was no means of traversing it, that is, of moving it from left to right and back again. It was in short a siege piece rather than a field piece. The length of the barrel was ten feet, the thickness of the metal at the muzzle, which was shaped crudely in the form of a dragon's or devil's head and mouth, was six inches and the aperture at the muzzle so big that a boy of four or five could sit in the mouth, though no boy could be found in the whole dukedom who would dare to try. It was met at the foot of the pass by the men of Grand Fenwick, Sir Roger among them, and these took possession there, and it was the labor of half a day to drag the huge piece of ordnance up the pass and get it into position before the castle.

With the cannon came fear. Fear walked foot by foot, like a shadow, with the monstrous engine of destruction as it was dragged into the little dukedom. Men called the cannon by common consent the Mouth of Hell, and while they labored with the horses which stumbled and slipped and plunged in their traces getting the cannon up the pass they kept glancing back at it. When they found the black mouth pointing at them, they shuddered and crossed themselves and contrived to move out of its line of fire. For they came to believe, just by looking at the cannon, that it had an explosive quality built into it—that at any moment, without human help, it would vomit a great sheet of fire which would reduce to a cinder anything in its path.

Normally at such arduous work there was much cheerful shouting and jeering and no small amount of swearing of a jovial sort. But in hauling the cannon there was a spell of silence upon the men of Grand Fenwick. They said little and much of what they said was prayer.

Even Sir Roger was for a while daunted when he saw the size of the piece. Such a large amount of metal in one piece—so thick and so long and so heavy—was in itself awesome. This thickness and strength of the metal was grim and mute testimony of the kind of destruction which the cannon generated in its bronze bowels to spew out of its mouth and destroy all who were near it. The cannon was bound around by huge hoops of iron—hoops far stronger than those which supported the hinges of the drawbridge of the castle of Grand Fenwick. Here again was evidence of violence such as these men had never looked upon before.

With the cannon came sixteen great stone balls—so big that only two might be supported on a cart. So it took eight carts to bring the missiles of the cannon into Grand Fenwick. And there were two other carts, these padded with leather, containing the barrels of gunpowder. Men looked then at the strength of the cannon and at the size of the stone balls, and at the cart all padded with leather and containing the gunpowder, and their hearts left them.

This was the new method of warfare. They took no courage from the possession of the cannon. The French, they had heard, had many of these engines and they were coming against Grand Fenwick with them. And they could see the whole dukedom going up in bloody slaughter and flames. They could, in short, see the end of the world insofar as they were concerned. And it would be a horrible end, comparable to a Biblical holocaust, against which they were quite helpless.

The day following the arrival of the cannon the people of Grand Fenwick were summoned by the ringing of the bell in the donjon keep of the castle to gather around the piece. The whole dukedom came—man, woman and child. But they would not approach near to the massive gun. They stood apart from it and stared at it and murmured. And little children who saw it burst unaccountably into tears and sought to hide behind their parents.

Sir Roger waddled boldly to the cannon, walked around it, put his hand down the mouth (which brought a low groan from the people) and then climbed atop the breech, from which vantage point he addressed his people.

"Here," he cried, "is an engine which it is claimed may blow down my castle and destroy my dukedom and my people. Mayhap it can. Mayhap the end has come to our freedom, for we can no longer defend ourselves with our bows. Yet I for one do not believe this. I believe man is superior to the works of man as a wheelwright is superior to his wheel and a soldier superior to his sword. For the power of the sword is the heart that wields it. And the power of this cannon lies in the courage of the men using it and the men who are opposed to it. If the men opposed are fearful—the cannon does not need even to be discharged. And I see by your attitudes now that if but three of these cannon pointed their mouths up the Pass of Pinot, there would not be many to challenge them, however bravely some of you spoke in the Council Chamber.

"Well, I do challenge this cannon. The lord Abbot hath all needed instructions upon how to load and fire it and that he will do and in a very little while. And I am going to mount upon the main keep of the castle, full in the field of the cannon's fire, and stay there while it is discharged.

"If I do not survive this test, then you may make whatever truce you wish with the French. If I do survive, then you will know that this cannon is not the all-powerful weapon you think it to be, and means may be devised of resisting it.

"Sir Dermot of Ballycastle will stand upon the main keep with me—having solicited the hand of the Lady Matilda. If he survives the test, he may have her hand. But I'll give my daughter to no man who is not prepared to face without flinching the direst perils which may confront this dukedom."

"My lord," said Bentner, approaching from the crowd, but not coming closer than fifteen paces to the cannon, "would it not be better to put this piece at the head of the pass so that it may be fired at the French as they come and so scatter them?"

"You mistake my point," said the Duke. "You would use the cannon for courage. If the cannon failed you, so would your courage. If you found four or five French cannon facing this one of ours, how many of you would remain in the fight? If some other weapon were devised more powerful yet than this (though it is hard to imagine such an invention) where would your courage be then, for you would not have this weapon? What I want to show you is that no weapon is of any use without a stout heart, and that a stout heart is on the other hand superior to any weapon likely to be invented. For weapons are all of them dependent upon men. And so long as men retain courage, so long will they survive free."

Having said this, which was somewhat more of a speech than he had intended, Sir Roger dismounted from the cannon, embraced the Lady Matilda, and with Sir Dermot walked across the courtyard and disappeared through the door at the base of the donjon keep.

The castle had been evacuated, and the cannon was placed outside its walls, but elevated at the main keep. In half an hour Sir Roger and Sir Dermot appeared here, having spent the time in getting into their armor. For Sir Roger insisted that they should be fully armored since they were knights and could not, without loss of dignity, appear for battle unarmored.

Over their heads, upon a flagpole between them, floated the banner of Grand Fenwick: the double-headed eagle saying "Aye" from one beak and "Nay" from the other. It occurred to Sir Roger, glancing up at it, that the emblem was indeed appropriate and that Grand Fenwick at that moment as well as he personally, stood on the verge of the greatest "Aye" or "Nay" with which it (or he) had ever been confronted.

Below them the crowd before the battlements were reduced to the size of pygmies, and in a huge clearing, and aimed directly at the two knights, so that they could see only the horrid "O" of its gaping mouth, was the cannon.

Sir Roger, surveying this scene, and conscious that he might have but a few moments left of life on earth, cast around in his mind for some words to say to the Irishman. But since he was of English stock he did not wish, even in the face of death, to say anything which might be construed as heroic lest he survive the ordeal and be ashamed of such an utterance. He cleared his throat once or twice, and then said:

"A fair day."

"So it was at Formigny," said Sir Dermot.

Sir Roger ignored this. He didn't want to discuss Formigny.

"I hope that damned Abbot knows what he is doing," he growled.

"And I," said Sir Dermot, "hope he doesn't."

"You are afraid, Sir Knight?" asked Sir Roger stiffly.

"I am," said the Irishman.

"Pshaw," said Sir Roger. "I know not the slightest fear."

"Then there's someone else with us," said Sir Dermot.

"How so?" demanded the Duke turning clumsily around.

"Because I hear armored knees knocking and mine are crossed," said the Irishman.

"It's my armor," said the Duke. "It fits poorly." He was silent for a while. "Actually," he said, "I am afraid."

"Then go down and stop it."

"Never," said the Duke. "Though you may leave if you wish."

"Never," said Sir Dermot.

For a while the two were silent.

"I do not remember," said the Duke at length, "the prayer to be said upon the eve of death."

"'Into Thy hands, O Lord, I commend my spirit. Lord Jesus receive my soul,'" said the Irishman.

"Sir Knight," said Sir Roger, "I would embrace you and ask that all bygones be forgotten, for it may be that we have not long to live."

The two placed their steel-bound arms about each other's steel-bound shoulders and then turned once more to face the cannon.

"You may fire, my lord Abbot," called Sir Roger, anticipating by a few centuries another famous command, "when you are ready."

But the lord Abbot was not yet ready.

He had put the contents of one of the barrels of gunpowder down the mouth of the cannon and, with the aid of four men whom he had first shriven and promised a full remission of all their sins for the service, had managed to roll one of the huge stone balls down on top of this. He had laid a train of powder upon several planks nailed end to end up to the touchhole of the gun so that he could fire the gun from the safe distance of three hundred feet. But now he wished to deliver a sermon upon the cannon. He bowed to the Duke and mounting upon a stand launched into his sermon, which was full of the threats of hell-fire and damnation for those who were remiss in their attendance at church or in the paying of their tithes for the support of God's ministry upon earth.

"There are some mockers," roared the Abbot in a voice which could be heard, though faintly, upon the battlements, "who doubt the existence of those eternal fires from which the wretches condemned for their sins can find no escape. There are some who say that the gates of Hell is but a phrase to frighten children and halfwits. Yet in a few moments you will see, my good people all, a little cracking as it were, a tiny opening, of those gates. You will see the fire burst forth where all now is serene. You will see the grasses devoured and hear the noise of the wrath of God. And when you see these things and hear these things, bear in mind that it is but a taste of the final opening of the gates of Hell at the Judgment Day and repent now while there is still time."

He stood erect and still for a moment and silence settled over the people; a silence which on the battlements was broken only by the muted flapping of the banner over the heads of the two knights; the banner with the enigmatic charge "Aye" and "Nay."

Then the Abbot got slowly down from his stand and walked to the end of the planks on which the train of powder had been laid. A groan went up from the crowd and the people started to move even farther back and spread outward from the cannon as leaves stirred by a puff of wind. Ten feet from the end of the powder trail was a brazier of glowing coals. The Abbot took a coal from this with a pair of long tongs, crossed himself, walked over to the powder, hesitated, squared his shoulders and then set the coal to the powder.

There was a hiss as of a serpent disturbed in some dark copse. A trail of smoke walked quite slowly up the planks, hesitating in places and then darting forward and then hesitating until it reached the head of the plank.

And then there came a mighty roar which rang backward and forward between the mountain peaks around, and with this roar a wall of flame, red and orange, flashed around the cannon and chunks of earth and lumps of iron were flung up into the air and came down in a vicious, erratic rain.

The crowd fled, those of them who had not been knocked to the ground by the shock of the explosion. Only the Abbot held his ground. He had put his arms up before his eyes and lowered them now. He looked first at the battlements. There were Sir Roger and Sir Dermot, standing as staunch as ever, their broadswords before them, and over them the flag.

Then he looked at the cannon. There was no cannon. Where the cannon had been there was a hole ripped in the earth big enough to bury a horse.

"Lord," said the Abbot crossing himself and falling devoutly to his knees, "I thank Thee humbly that I have not destroyed my liege lord nor the beloved of my lady." Still on his knees he looked around once more at the two on the battlements and at the mammoth strength of the castle of Grand Fenwick, at once the symbol of the Duchy's strength and the source of its government. He sensed that had the cannon breached the walls of the castle, the people of Grand Fenwick would have known that their old form of government, so suited to their needs, could no longer be maintained.

"Lord," he continued, "I have worked a deceit upon these people but for their good. It was necessary to restore their courage by blowing up this engine. Be with them in the hour of battle when the French come. Strengthen their hearts and let them dispatch to Thy gates such a host of Frenchmen that we may, in future, be left here in peace to continue in our own ways. Amen."

The people returned only slowly to the scene of the explosion. They looked in amazement at the huge hole in the ground and at the grass around it which was blacked by fire and still burning in parts.

"Well," demanded the Abbot, "what do you think of this weapon now? Who is it the more likely to destroy—the French or us?"

"'Tis certain," said Robin Goodspeed, "that no man may seek

to tame the powers of Hell except at his own peril."

"I believe," said the Abbot, "that you speak more truly than you know."

Sir Roger, when he got down from the battlements, was inclined to be angry with the Abbot for overcharging the cannon with gunpowder, for he was not so simple as to believe that it had blown up because it was, in itself, an unreliable weapon. But the Abbot mollified him readily enough.

"Your Grace," he said, "you are yourself the principal weapon of the dukedom. It is better that you should be preserved and the cannon destroyed, than that you should be dead and the cannon still with us. Cannons cannot lead men, Your Grace."

"I would still have liked to know whether it could breach the walls of the castle," said Sir Roger grumpily.

"It could have knocked such a hole in the wall," said Sir Dermot, "as no mason could ever repair. But let us fall now to perfecting our plans to deal with the French. And in those plans I now claim the right to take part, though ignored in the past."

"In the past you were not of Grand Fenwick," replied the Duke.

"That is mended now," replied the Irishman. "Here is me plot of land and I will either prevail with it or fall with it, and the test is likely to come within the week."

CHAPTER XVII

THE army of the King of France, when it left Paris, numbered twenty thousand men. It was led by Dunois the sturdy Bastard of Orleans and the Constable, Richemont. It included a host of several hundred knights together with their squires and armorers and their servants, and an artillery train of fifteen cannon.

The artillery train was the most formidable part of the army. The gunners were all dressed in bright red. The color was adopted to warn the rest of the army of the danger of the artillery and particularly of the barrels of gunpowder which the gunners carried with them. The artillery train was compelled, for reasons of safety, to camp two hundred paces apart from the rest of the army each night. In their red clothing, the gunners looked like so many devils, or so many executioners, and even among the French, they were avoided.

The artillery train, though of but fifteen cannon at the start of the march south to Grand Fenwick, was certainly the most cumbersome section of the French host. Each gun required six or more horses to haul it forward on its cart or sled. Then there was the ammunition train, the heavy wains laden with cannon balls or gun stones and others, packed with straw, which contained the barrels of gunpowder. All these carts and the draft animals required a small army of drivers to handle them. And with the artillery came also the servants of the gunners who cooked for them and fed the animals and helped when a cart or cannon fell into one of the potholes which bestrewed every road of France.

Because of the unwieldiness of the artillery, progress south was at the rate of but eight miles a day. But at the end of each day the army had swollen in numbers, some of the addition being camp followers—the jackals of war. But many were knights summoned to join, each providing artillery of his own. Three thousand men and four cannon joined at Orleans, five thousand and four more cannon at Berry, two thousand and two cannon at March, eight thousand and six cannon at Lyonnais, so that the huge serpent of the French army, gliding slowly toward the tiny mouse of Grand Fenwick, grew longer and longer. It was a serpent with a silver head, formed of the armored knights, and a scarlet tail, made up of the artillery train. It spread over a distance of ten miles and was the wonder of all France. The noise of its approach could be heard before the first of its banners appeared in sight. And as this army moved it raised a cloud of dust which rose into the luminous French skies, glittering like a silver powder in the sunlight, and it could be seen from ten or fifteen miles away.

At Lyons assurances were sent to the Duke of Burgundy and to the Dauphin that the army marched not against either of them, but only against the Duchy of Grand Fenwick which lay between these two lands. Burgundy's reply brought a flush of anger to the French Constable. It was: "How weak is your king that he assembled such a host to stamp out an insect?" The Dauphin's reply was equally sarcastic. It was: "Does all France still tremble when an English churl fits an arrow to his bowstring?"

These replies rankled the more because in Berry a friar of Grand Fenwick, sent as an emissary of the Duchy to the French Constable, had presented him with a cloth-yard arrow with the warning to remember the past and stay clear of the Duchy.

The nobler elements of the French army felt themselves dishonored at the size of the force which was being brought against so tiny a foe, and swore that were it not that they owed military service to the King in return for their estates, they would not accompany the Constable. They also resented the care and the reliance which were vested in the artillery, for they felt that the peasants of the gunners' train—men without title or land or noble heritage—were set above themselves, and the honor of a victory would go to them, and that they, the knights, were attendants upon the scarlet gunners and their cumbersome cannon.

Added to this was the fact that the progress of the knights had to be slowed to the pace of eight miles a day, which was all the artillery train could accomplish. Thus there was considerable quarreling among the French, whose knights grew to loathe the artillery which laid them open to every kind of ridicule. Dunois and the Constable were besieged with requests to let the knights go ahead and deal with Grand Fenwick.

But on this score, Dunois, well versed in war, refused to budge.

All he would permit was that the mounted men should be permitted to ride ahead of the artillery train but must make camp each day at a place where the gunners could catch up with them. And they were, under no circumstances, arriving at the Pass of Pinot ahead of the artillery, to open battle with Grand Fenwick. They must wait until the artillery had arrived and the pieces were ready to be hauled into the pass to blast a way into Grand Fenwick for the horsemen.

In Grand Fenwick, meanwhile, every man, woman and child in the Duchy was at work preparing for the great battle for survival. Spies brought to Sir Roger almost daily reports on the advance of the French, and on these reports he estimated that the French would be at the foot of the pass on the third Friday in August.

To prepare for battle much that was old was done and much also that was new. Among the old preparations was the storing of the castle itself with great quantities of food to prepare for a siege and the assigning of all the people of Grand Fenwick living space within the castle. All would withdraw to the castle on the day before the arrival of the French, except the eight hundred men and boys who comprised the pygmy army of the tiny Duchy. All of these—including Sir Roger—were bowmen.

There were, as noted previously, but five men in the Duchy of the degree of knight, to whom was now added Sir Dermot. This half dozen could not properly be used as cavalry in the traditional manner, nor could they be used for the protection of the bowmen, guarding their flanks. For three armored men on each side of a company of eight hundred can scarcely be counted a flank guard. Each, however, was given command of a company of a hundred and sixty bowmen, with Sir Roger in over-all command of the Grand Fenwick army.

Three of these companies of a hundred and sixty, under the command of Sir Derek of Azule, Sir William of Azule and the Count of Mountjoy, were situated deep in the pass, blocking the end where it debouched into the dukedom proper. They drove stakes into the ground, with pointed ends directed down the pass, as a protection against the French horse, and they were grouped behind these stakes. Sir Dermot insisted that the ground behind the stakes be scooped out in a broad trench and the bowmen be stationed there behind a breastwork of earth. Sir Roger thought this sacrilege and opposed the idea violently. He said it smacked of cowardice, for it would make it appear that the bowmen of Grand Fenwick were not prepared to stand in plain sight of their enemy, but were hiding from them in the ground.

Sir Dermot, however, pointed out that should the French succeed in getting their cannon to this part of the pass, the bowmen would be protected by the trench and earthworks from the cannon shot and could still use their weapons. And since the Abbot warmly supported Sir Dermot, this use of trench warfare—one of the first on record—was agreed.

The Pass of Pinot might be thought of as a breach in the mountain walls which guarded the Duchy of Grand Fenwick. The entrance to the pass was a wide funnel where the Alps petered off into thin foothills. It was not possible with so few men to make any defense of this area. But there came one point where the pass struggled upward until for the space of a hundred yards it was no more than fifty yards wide, with sheer rocky slopes on either side. Sir Roger had wanted to block this off completely before the coming of the French—in short to seal the pass against them, for his military thinking was conditioned by castles. If there was a breach in a castle wall, the plain answer was to seal the breach.

Here again Sir Dermot differed with him. He saw immediately the advantage of this narrow neck of the pass, but proposed that it should be left open until the French army had halfway advanced into it. Then it should be closed to cut the French force in two, severing the rear guard from the advance guard.

"And how are we to close it in the middle of the battle?" demanded Sir Roger heatedly.

"With gunpowder," replied Sir Dermot. "Faith we've enough of it left to blow down a mountain." He then explained that it should be possible, by driving tunnels into either side of the narrow part of the pass, and putting gunpowder at the ends of these tunnels, to blow up the walls of the pass, and send an avalanche of rocks cascading down upon the French from both sides. This also was new to Sir Roger— the use of stone avalanches as weapons, but he agreed to the measure.

Two companies of bowmen were to be situated on either side of the bottleneck. One would be under the command of Sir Dermot and the other under the command of the Count of Azules. Sir Roger, standing apart upon a rock pinnacle, would be in a position to survey the whole battle and would have with him Nicholas Breakspear to act as a messenger.

On the morning of the third Friday of August the French reached the mouth of the pass. Their progress had been watched the previous day and Sir Roger was enormously proud at the size of the force sent against him. They encamped that night, Thursday night, at the mouth of the funnel, and were up with the sun on the morning of Friday.

All in Grand Fenwick were ready. The women and children were inside the castle. The drawbridge was pulled up and the portcullis lowered. In the field alone were the eight hundred of Grand Fenwick, the archers standing at their posts with huge tubs containing sheaves of arrows beside them. Each bowman had a short sword and a buckler. But these they had laid upon the ground to leave their bow arms free. They wore no uniform, these archers, only the clothing of their trade—blacksmith's apron or a plowman's jerkin, a shepherd's fleece coat or a cowherd's rude surcoat of leather. Only the knights bore charges—the twins of Azule surcoats quartered with blue lozenges, Mountjoy with a blazon of a burning bush, and Sir Dermot (at the insistence of Sir Roger) a very tattered surcoat of a salmon gules in a field argent (though the argent was badly in need of a wash, being more gray than silver).

The Abbot stood beside Sir Roger, his gown over a suit of armor whose straps could hardly be made to meet. He had had a battle with his conscience for some days, for he was forbidden, as a man of the cloth, to shed blood with the sword. On the other hand, the mace, permitted to him, he concluded would be of little use. So he had equipped himself with a longbow, arguing that Christ in admonishing Peter to put up his sword had said nothing about the use of bows. Behind Sir Roger, on a flagpole, fluttered the double-headed eagle of Grand Fenwick, asking its traditional question "Aye" or "Nay."

A herald first approached from the French lines, protected from injury by his tabard, the badge of his office, and Sir Roger left his position atop the rock pinnacle to meet him. The herald demanded that Sir Roger surrender himself to the mercy of the French king. Sir Roger replied he would sooner surrender to the mercy of the Devil. He offered a counter-proposal that Dunois meet him in personal combat, and let them decide the issue and so save the blood of many who would otherwise fall. This offer was rejected within the hour and the French then moved from their encampment, up the pass.

They came with their cavalry in the lead, for these would on no account be persuaded to follow after the artillery. And there being so many French knights, they had drawn lots to decide who among them, out of the ten thousand now gathered for the assault, should actually take part in it.

Two thousand were chosen and these, their banners flapping

bravely in the wind, detached themselves from the main army and came slowly and menacingly up the pass.

Their armor glittered with diamond points of light in the sun and their surcoats, brave with the proud charges of France, were as bright as a field of poppies as they pressed forward. None hindered them as they progressed into the narrowing funnel and when they were two hundred paces from the narrowest part, they closed their visors, brought down their lances and with a cry of "St. Denis! St. Denis!" clapped spurs to their charges and thundered into the gorge.

Stones clattered from beneath the hoofs of the horses, knight jostled knight, plumes streamed from their helmets, and still not an arrow was loosed. They roared through the pass and found no enemy standing there. Those in the van concluded that the army of Grand Fenwick was cooped up inside the castle and so their brave charge was in vain. The foremost reined in their horses, those to the rear bounced into them, and the horsemen milled around beyond the bottleneck in a turmoil, shouting at each other. A second charge of the French came up the pass five minutes after the first, for those who had not been included by the lots cast thought it small honor to play at dice and cards when there might be other sport to be had. These mingled in the turmoil created by the reining in of the first charge. No one had clear command, for the Constable, who had led the first charge, could not make himself heard in the hubbub and in any case had not expected to have to give verbal commands in the midst of the battle.

He did see, about a quarter of a mile away, a number of stakes driven in the ground and a mound of earth, but there were no archers in sight near these as was usually the case, and altogether he did not know what to make of the situation.

He with other members of the first charge, were driven by the arrival of the second in the constricted area to spread out toward the farther end of the pass within a few hundred yards of the stakes, but still he saw nothing.

Then from behind the French horse there was suddenly an earth-shaking roar and a massive volume of rocks and earth and limbs of trees was flung into the air and with it a monstrous cloud of dust. This was so unexpected, and its effect so magnified by the mountains around, that the horses were immediately panicked. They bucked and swerved and started forward and pranced, flinging their riders to the ground. And in the same moment there came from the stakes and mounds of earth the Constable had noted, a storm of arrows. These, tipped with an inch of fire-hardened steel, flung down in a deadly rain upon the surging, whirling mass of the French knights, striking them and their steeds to the ground.

None among the French knew what was the cause of the violent explosion behind. They could see no foe ahead. They rode each other down, lances snapping, swords flaying, and scores falling from their horses were trampled to death upon the ground.

Still the arrows came at intervals of six seconds between flights—arrows bunched in a phalanx of steel, and driven with the force of seventy-pound bows. Those in the van of the French, exposed to this fire, sought to drive to the rear. Those in the rear, of whom some hundreds had been killed by the explosion in the gorge, or buried under the debris, sought to drive to the front. And men, heavy-armored and caught in panic, exhausted themselves in a few minutes of senseless jostling out of which no order could be obtained.

And still the merciless arrows came with machine-like precision—came from nowhere and riddled knights and horses so that many fell to the ground as full of arrows as a pincushion is of pins.

The explosion in the neck of the pass had brought down a ponderous fall of rock and earth which formed a barrier about twelve feet high in the middle and perhaps six feet broad, cutting the pass in two. Sir Roger on one side with the Count of Azule had a hundred and sixty bowmen, and Sir Dermot on the other side, a like amount as noted. These had so far taken no part in the battle.

Sir Dermot now detached a hundred of his men to move down the pass to where the French cavalry were milling around, and these loosed their arrows in the mass of the French. The Count of Azule followed this example, so that the bottled-up French horse were stricken from ahead and from both sides. They might, could any order have been brought to them, have charged the bowmen ahead and, by the force of the charge, won through their tormenters. But they were beyond order, and untrained in real cavalry tactics and so remained to be slaughtered.

Behind the barrier caused by the explosion, Dunois had remained, and discovering what had taken place, and that his army was split in two with the artillery in the rear, he ordered the area cleared and twelve of the heaviest cannon brought forward. These were dragged with infinite labor toward the narrow part of the pass. There they were to open fire upon the barrier of earth and rocks and make a breach in it through which the rear part of the French might stream to unite with their fellows ahead.

Sir Dermot now raised upon a pole a strip of red cloth, this being a signal previously agreed with the Count of Azule on the opposite wall. He and the Count had provided themselves with buckets of hot oil and a large quantity of rags, and the time had come to put these curious weapons to use. Each of their archers tied a wad of rag to the head of an arrow, dipped it in the oil and set it alight in a brazier of coals. And the arrows trailing a curious plume of black smoke were now loosed at the wagons containing the store of French powder.

In his anxiety to effect a breach in the barrier as soon as possible, Dunois had made the error of bringing his ammunition wagons within range of these arrows. He realized his mistake too late. A flock of fifty or sixty arrows with burning tows at their heads plumped into the barrels of gunpowder on the wains. The red-jacketed gunners saw them and fled. Seconds later first one and then another and then three and then half a dozen barrels of gunpowder exploded. The whole ammunition train erupted in a sustained roar which filled the bottom of the pass with orange flames. Men and animals shrieked in their death agonies and the remainder of the French host, seeing the floor of the valley converted into a lake of fire, seeing the red gunners rushing down upon them, turned and fled.

Some of the guns which had been dragged forward to the barrier had been loaded, though their gunners left them when they saw the burning arrows plump into the gunpowder wagons. These guns now discharged. The first two or three discharged, knocked a breach in the barrier, and the other guns, going off, flung their gun stones and metal shot into what was left of the French on the other side.

The whole action lasted but half an hour. And what had started out as a perfectly planned and controlled battle on the part of the French Constable and Dunois, with an army outnumbering the men of Grand Fenwick forty to one, was turned into a bloody and burning shambles out of which no order could be summoned.

An attempt was made by some of the French knights, shamed into action by Dunois, to rescue the guns. But they found them upended and found also that the draft animals for hauling them were dead or terribly wounded. And so the guns had to remain where they were, and Dunois took it upon himself to sound a parley.

Accompanied by his herald, he plodded up the side of the pass to where Sir Roger stood upon his rock pinnacle and bluntly conceded the day to Grand Fenwick. He asked an end to the fighting so that the dead might be buried.

From the eminence on which the parley took place, Dunois could see past the barrier to the area where the French horse had been trapped. The scene chilled even the veteran warrior of Orleans.

The floor of the valley was littered with men and horses, piled upon each other like logs or boulders. Few of the French knights remained mounted. It was impossible to ride a horse through the litter of the dead and wounded. Beyond he saw the bowmen of Grand Fenwick—and was astonished that there were so few. There were, in fact, but four hundred and eighty of them under Sir William and Sir Derek of Azule and the old Count of Mountjoy. Yet this small body had loosed an astonishing quantity of arrows—nearly five hundred every five seconds, making a rate of six thousand arrows a minute. And since the action had lasted for half an hour, some hundred and eighty thousand arrows had been loosed into five thousand of the French in a confined area. That any survived at all could be regarded as wonderful. The arrows lay about like jackstraws, and in the clear light it was possible to pick out men with four or five goose-quill shafts piercing them.

"You have destroyed," Dunois said to Sir Roger, "some of the boldest men of France."

"I sent you one arrow," replied the Duke, "and you took no heed. Perhaps now you have had arrows enough. If not we have many more, for the men of my dukedom have been making these for the past month or more."

"We have had a surfeit," said Dunois.

The tally of the casualties was thirteen thousand of the French killed or wounded and none of Grand Fenwick.

The peace parley was short and after it the French withdrew while Sir Roger consulted with his council as to the terms of the victory. He demanded neither booty nor captives from them. There was some argument in the council that it might be well to keep the French cannon but the Abbot persuaded against this.

"These cannon," he said, "will in time be out of date, and other weapons will take their place which we can by no means afford in Grand Fenwick. Let us stick to our longbows. With them we can defend the dukedom, and none will surely believe that we intend to invade the territory of others. If we mass other kinds of armament, there may be some suspicion that we are ambitious for more territory, and that will bring war upon our heads."

Later this counsel of the Abbot's was incorporated in a solemn declaration of the Freemen of Grand Fenwick. This declaration stated that the national weapon of the Duchy was and always would remain the longbow which had many times proved sufficient for the defense of the land.

The declaration continued, that no other weapon, however improved or powerful, should ever be adopted by the Duchy, for it would be more than was needed for defense and so would arouse suspicion that Grand Fenwick was preparing for a war of aggression.

As for the French, a treaty was drawn up guaranteeing that the King of France would never again come against Grand Fenwick and recognizing the independence of the dukedom. This pact, called the Treaty of the Pass of Pinot, was signed in a somewhat curious form by Sir Roger. Instead of writing his name he drew a sketch of an arrow and remarked grimly that such a signature could likely compel better observance of the pact than any other he could think of.

History records that this was so, for there were no further attacks by France upon the dukedom.

CHAPTER XVIII

AFTER the battle came the wedding of Sir Dermot and the Lady Matilda. It was held in the Great Hall of the castle and attended by Lords and Commons, and was magnificent. The Lady Matilda wore a horned hennin of mild blue, covered with a veil of pale gold lace and houppelande of white watered silk with a floral design of blue worked into it. She looked like an angel appearing upon earth to take part in a beautiful masque.

Sir Dermot of Ballycastle had been magnificently fitted out in a brave cotehardie of scarlet, and particolored trunk hose. He had further been given an excellent cap, made in the fashion of a turban with a flash of pleated red cloth escaping from the center.

All agreed that he was a striking figure but none would say that he was handsome. His big mustaches still had the look of dogs' tails to them, his knees were somewhat knobbly in his trunk hose and his shoulders were rounded. He was still the most unlikely figure of a knight Grand Fenwick had ever seen. But Grand Fenwick had now taken him to its heart, and rejoiced that when the evil day came and Sir Roger was no longer with them, Sir Dermot would be Duke and the Lady Matilda Duchess of Grand Fenwick.

For the wedding service, Nicholas Breakspear had composed a hymn of love of great simplicity and tenderness. This was sung, after the Abbot had blessed the couple, by a choir of monks and boys, for the hymn had been arranged for five voices and the blending of the piping notes of the boys with the deep bass of the monks was moving in the extreme.

A guard of honor of bowmen formed outside the Great Hall to see the couple off on their honeymoon which was spent in Switzerland, and during the absence of his daughter and his son-in-law, Sir Roger daily climbed to the top of the donjon keep as was his custom. But now his eyes were no longer turned to the French lands but to that pass into Switzerland whence the Lady Matilda and Sir Dermot would be returning. And when they returned he gave a great banquet, and to show the great esteem in which he now held the Irishman, his son-in-law, he asked him to recite all seventy verses of the ballad which Sir Dermot had composed when leaving England for the Battle of Formigny and of which he had recited but one verse to Sir Roger upon their first meeting.

To be sure Sir Roger fell asleep in the middle of the twelfth verse, but, as Breakspear said, six verses of poetry were the equivalent of a hard day's riding for the Duke.

When all had settled down to normal in Grand Fenwick, Sir Dermot one day called Breakspear and told him that he wished to send him on an important mission to Ireland.

"And what is the mission, my dear lord?" asked the Lady Matilda, busy with a piece of needlework.

"I have been thinking, me love," said Sir Dermot, "of me old friend Sir Kevin of Rathgorm and his seventeen daughters. And I have been reflecting that we have in the duchy two unwed knights without any lady to champion other than the Lady Janice. And I do not want the next knight who comes through Grand Fenwick to be put to the trouble I was meself in almost the same circumstances. Therefore, I am going to ask me friend Sir Kevin to send me two of his daughters for these two good knights and in this way will promote the peace of the duchy, add to the noble stock of the land, and relieve the burdens of me poor friend."

"Poor Lady Janice," said the Lady Matilda with a wistful smile. "She will have no knight of her own."

"Don't fret about her for a moment," said Sir Dermot. "For I have persuaded your father to dub Master Nicholas knight, and since he has long fretted for the hand of the Lady Janice, though afraid to plead his suit, because of his low degree, all will soon be well there."

"Master Nicholas a knight?" said the Lady Matilda. "Is it for brave behavior at the Pass of Pinot? I had not heard that he had distinguished himself."

"No," said Sir Dermot. "It is not."

"Then what service hath he done to warrant this elevation?"

"He once, though trembling with fear, struck me a buffet in defense of his lady," said Sir Dermot, "and in this he displayed the first quality of Knighthood, which is not to be unafraid, but to overcome fear in a good cause."

He pulled at his long mustaches and eyed the needlework in the Lady Matilda's hands. "I fancy, me dear," he said, "that you are making there a very small shirt!"

"I am," said the Lady Matilda, blushing.

"We'll call him Brian," said Sir Dermot. "Sir Brian of Ballycastle and Grand Fenwick. I must see about getting him a good horse. It's well known in Ireland that a boy is never too young for a horse."

BOOKS IN THE GRAND FENWICK SERIES
Available for the first time on eBooks

Books 2 through 5 are best read after *The Mouse That Roared*, but all of the books can be read and enjoyed at any point in the series.

The Mouse That Roared (Book 1)

The Mouse On The Moon (Book 2)

The Mouse On Wall Street (Book 3)

The Mouse That Saved The West (Book 4)

Beware of The Mouse (A Prequel to *The Mouse That Roared*) *(Book 5)*

THE FATHER BREDDER MYSTERIES
Now Available Exclusively on Kindle

Named "A Red Badge Novel of Suspense" alongside Agatha Christie, Michael Innes, and Hugh Pentecost, *The Father Bredder Mysteries*, written by Leonard Wibberley under the pen name Leonard Holton.

Father Joseph Bredder was a decorated sergeant in the U.S. Marine Corps. before becoming a Franciscan priest and amateur detective who both solves crimes and saves souls.

When Father Bredder gets involved with murder—Heaven only knows what will happen next…

"Amazing."
—LOS ANGELES HERALD EXPRESS

"Absorbing Mystery."
—LEWISTON JOURNAL

"Fast moving action … Father Bredder exercises his very special talents against extreme odds to solve a baffling mystery."
—HARTFORD COURANT

The Father Bredder Mystery Series

The Saint Maker
A Pact with Satan
Secret of the Doubting Saint
Deliver Us from Wolves
Flowers by Request
Out of the Depths
A Touch of Jonah
A Problem in Angels
The Mirror of Hell
The Devil to Play
A Corner of Paradise

THE CENTURION
A Roman Soldier's Testament of the Passion of Christ
Available for the first time on eBooks

Each of the first three Gospels calls attention to the Roman centurion—Longinus—who officiated at the Crucifixion, and it is through the life-changing story of this duty-bound soldier that Leonard Wibberley achieves, with a shrewd appreciation of human motives, a thoroughly fresh interpretation of the Gospel story of Christ's ministry and Passion.

★★★★★

"It is a very moving, delicately constructed novel, with a wonderful feeling for the dawn of Christianity in the Roman world."
—*Amazon Reviewer*

FLINT'S ISLAND
The Lost Sequel to *Treasure Island*
Available for the first time on eBooks

An unofficial sequel to the most popular pirate tale ever told— Robert Louis Stevenson's *Treasure Island*.

In this story inspired by the opening line of the famous novel, in which Jim Hawkins tells of a "treasure not yet lifted" still hidden on an unknown island, find out what became of literature's most beloved "bad guy"—Long John Silver—and whatever happened to the remaining treasure.

"Silver's wiliness and Flint's mystique are perfectly captured and the American seamen—prudent Captain Samuels, the unimaginative Yankee carpenter Smigley, the impulsive mutineer Green and the loyal, but mean-spirited Peasbody are worthy of their *Hispaniola* counterparts."
—*Kirkus Reviews*

McGILLICUDDY McGOTHAM
Special 60ᵗʰ Anniversary Edition
Available for the first time on eBooks

From the bestselling author of *The Mouse That Roared* comes a witty tale of a leprechaun in New York. Timothy Patrick Fergus Kevin Sean Desmond McGillicuddy (for short) is a leprechaun diplomat on a mission to convince the President of the United States to halt the construction of a new U.S.-owned airport on a tract of Little People land in Ireland. With the belief "mischief is me nature" and the help of a 10-year-old American boy, he proves wee folk a big force to be reckoned with.

This special anniversary edition features a new Introduction by journalist and author Quentin Fottrell, Rosalind Russell memorabilia, and previously unpublished photos of the author. A timeless classic, *McGillicuddy McGotham* will charm adults & young readers alike.

"Leonard Wibberley is that rare writer who can combine satire and fantasy and humor and storytelling, and who can write with equal appeal for young readers and adults. All his special abilities and his good qualities combine in this fanciful tale"—*Los Angeles Times*

THE BALLAD OF THE PILGRIM CAT
A Thanksgiving Poem for Children

In a moment of weakness, Leonard Wibberley once brought home a kitten for his daughter only to realize he was allergic to cats. He wrote this whimsically humorous Thanksgiving poem about a young pilgrim girl and the raffish cat she adopts after it stows away on the *Mayflower* with an inhaler by his typewriter and a curse on his lips.

"It is a family tradition to read this every Thanksgiving Day at our house. A treasure!"—*Google Books Reviewer*

Download the FREE 22-minute MP3 audiobook read by Leonard Wibberley himself at http://bit.ly/PilgrimKat

ABOUT THE AUTHOR

Leonard Wibberley was born in Dublin Ireland, in 1915. He was the sixth child of a schoolteacher and an agricultural scientist. When he was nine, his family moved to London. Seven years later, when his father died, he went to work as a stockroom apprentice for a publisher and later became a reporter. After various jobs, he came to the United States in 1943 and engaged in newspaper work for ten years. While working for the Los Angeles Times, he published his first work, *The King's Beard*. Three years later, he published his most successful book, *The Mouse That Roared*, which was serialized in *The Saturday Evening Post*, and later made into a classic film starring Peter Sellers.

Wibberley lived in Hermosa Beach from 1949 until his death in 1983. With his wife, Hazel, who clean typed his work, they raised six children and wrote over 100 books and hundreds of newspaper articles.

Check out his website at:

http://leonardwibberley.wix.com/author

Sign up for our monthly newsletter to receive columns written by Leonard Wibberley that were syndicated by newspapers nationally over his lifetime:

http://bit.ly/LeonardNews

You will also receive news of the upcoming releases of the ebook and paperback editions of his many novels, including his series of Father Bredder murder mysteries.

Made in United States
Orlando, FL
22 December 2021